1

The Diary of Miss Ruby March

Elizabeth Manning-Ives

The Diary of Miss Ruby March

Published by Woodlark Publishing
Copyright © Elizabeth Manning-Ives
ISBN-13: 9780993349195
ISBN-10: 0993349195

The Diary of Miss Ruby March

Acknowledgements

Grateful Thanks to:

Hope Watson for allowing me to use her photograph
for the cover of this book.

Catherine Quinlan for all her hard work and assistance
in preparing this book for publication and for
encouraging me to believe in myself.

Everyone at the Beccles Creative Writing and Pen To
Paper for all their support and encouragement through
some challenging times.

All at Twyfords in Beccles for their welcome, and for
providing excellent refreshments.

The Diary of Miss Ruby March

18 August 1876

As a young child I can remember always dreaming of living in a house surrounded by mountains. I always thought of the freedom and romance it would bring. Now at the age of just fourteen, following years of being moved from one place to another, from one set of people to another, I am finally going somewhere that I might eventually be able to call home. At the moment I only know the name of the house and the family who live there. I will not find out where it is until all the necessary arrangements have been made. I just know that to finally belong somewhere is exciting, and I cannot wait to be there.

My first two years I am told, were spent with my mother, who I have no memory of, apart from the day I was taken to live with my Aunt and Uncle. One haunting image has remained with me all these years and I cannot even be certain if it is real, or my earliest experience of escaping into my imagination. But, whenever I think back, I always see an image of a tear-stained face leaning towards me, before feeling the gentlest of kisses on my forehead as I am snatched up and put into the care of people, who apparently had no more choice in this than I did. I have no real memory of this time either, except that it was not a happy time for me at all. I know I was treated like an unwanted burden rather than a niece, often being locked alone in the attic for hours. My only friend during this time was a servant girl called Elsie who only appeared when I was four. She used to sneak up to see me every day, bringing me a treat from the kitchen, or a flower from the garden. If it had not been for Elsie and her visits in my last two years here, I am sure I would not have survived.

At the age of only six I found myself being sent away again, only this time it was to a huge, dark, scary building, I was told it was a school. My time there was equally as miserable, crying myself to sleep every night and constantly finding myself in trouble; I found myself being blamed, even when whatever had happened was nothing to do with me. I have always had a vivid imagination, and often found myself creating stories to comfort myself, and eventually several of the other girls at school too. But this also proved to cause me trouble. I would often get caught daydreaming in lessons, or find myself late for class because I was too busy creating my own little world; a world where I was safe and loved, not punished and locked away. Instead I was often scolded for being inattentive and disobedient.

'Ruby March! That imagination of yours must be curbed. It will only get you into trouble. Girls like you need to learn their place!'
Then chores would be forced on me, both before and after lessons.

'You will continue to be punished this way until you have learned your lesson and those silly stories are forgotten!'

I never truly discovered what this lesson was; but by the time I crawled into my bed each night, I was far too exhausted to imagine anything. Then, at the age of ten, I once again found myself being uprooted and sent to another new place. This continued until now, each one worse than the one before.

I often asked about my mother, but this only brought on either a sharp tongued response, or more often a beating.

'Don't be such an ungrateful little wretch! You don't know how lucky you are not to be with her. You were taken from the gutter so you didn't end up like her. She was no good do you hear? No good! Now let that be an end to your constant questioning you little guttersnipe!'

After this I stopped asking, but I have

never stopped thinking about her. Had she ever really loved me I'd wonder? Was I given away, so that I might have a better life? Or was I just taken from her? Was she even still alive?

By this time my imagination had all but completely abandoned me, or so I thought.

At fourteen years of age, I find myself sitting in a long dark corridor, awaiting my fate, and instead of dreading this next move, I am looking forward to it. For the first time in a long while something inside me is beginning to stir, almost reawakening me, it is as if something is already calling to me.

Three other girls are sitting with me, but none of us dare speak for fear of being heard. Idle chatter is certainly not approved of in this place. The door opens, we all flinch and one of the other girls is called through. She enters the room; the large heavy oak door closes behind her with a loud echoing boom. The three of us that remain, sit staring at each other. Each of us known to the other, but real friendship isn't easy in this place. Silent still, tentative smiles and knowing looks pass between the three of us. Time creeps so slowly, like the constant slow drip from a tap, but the huge grandfather clock shows, only a few minutes elapse.

The Diary of Miss Ruby March

The door opens again, this time my name is called out. I stand, begin to walk solemnly towards the open door, but the closer I get the more I tighten inside. I tremble as the matron stands impatiently and stern-looking in the doorway.

'Hurry up there girl, we haven't got all day you know!'

Saying nothing, I quicken my pace and enter the room. The heavy door almost slams shut behind me. I'm trapped! I can feel my heart pounding in my chest.

'Sit down girl, and be quick about it.'

With my legs rapidly getting weaker and more wobbly, I gratefully obey Matron's latest order. As she takes her seat behind the large dark wood desk, a thin weasel-featured man begins to speak.

'Ruby March, you are here today because you are to leave us at the end of the summer. Your new home is to be many miles from here in the far north of England. I understand you already know the place is called 'Valley Manor', and that the name of the family is Haskell, but now you know where you are going also. You are to travel to Penrith by train, from where you will be collected and taken to the Manor. You will make your journey on the first day of

September, and are to be taken on as a lady's maid for the youngest daughter, Miss Florence Haskell. The Haskell's are a very well-known and well-respected family up there, so remember to mind your manners, work hard, hold your tongue, and most importantly of all, keep your opinions to yourself! Is that clear?'

The three people sitting behind the huge desk are so severe, I feel my lip begin to quiver, I fear I may cry, but manage to answer without too much of a wobble in my voice.

'Good! Now, you will be provided with three outfits when you leave here which are to be kept neat and tidy at all times. You will receive one uniform, one plain but serviceable day dress and one which is to be kept for best. You will also receive a cape, bonnet and gloves to travel in and use whenever you need to leave the house. Never forget you have been given this chance as a student of this school, so to be properly attired will ensure you do not dishonour this establishment, its officers or yourself! Your clothes will be packed and ready for you to take when you leave. Do you understand everything you have been told today?'

'Yes sir.'

'You may leave us now and return to

your duties.'

I rise from the chair and walk towards the large wooden door once more as matron opens it; her scathing tone pursues me along the corridor.

'No dawdling now, straight to the workroom, do you hear me?'

'Yes Ma'am'

'Well see that you do it. I will be checking with your teacher later!'

My heart sinks as I make my way back along the corridor to the workroom. My teacher is worse than matron. Now I am leaving, I know she will do everything in her power to make my life even more unbearable. Just like I have seen it so often with girls before me.

As soon as I arrive at the workroom my worst fears are confirmed.

'Well, here at last I see! Miss Ruby March has decided to honour us with her presence after all? Well don't stand there girl get to work, just because you are moving on soon doesn't mean you don't have to work. In fact, it is all the more reason why you should work even harder! You wretched little baggages, when the time comes for you to move on, you seem to think that the rest of your time here doesn't matter. Well let me dispel that illusion immediately. Your work here will not end until the day you leave, and then you will find out what real work is, and just how hard life can really be.'

I make my way to my usual seat at the back of the room and take out my work from my desk. However, before I can even begin stitching my teacher is yelling my name once more.

'Ruby March! What makes you think you can just sit yourself at the back there? Bring your work up to me for inspection immediately; I need to check it before you make even more of a mess of it.'

As I make my way forward once more, I can feel my face burn; my eyes sting, but know I cannot afford to let it show. Previous to moving into this class, I have always been told that my work was neat and tidy, now, even the slightest error is heralded as evil and some form of punishment allotted.

Before I can even hand my work over, it is snatched from my grasp, I am sure I hear the fabric rip as it leaves my trembling hand.

'Hmm, well I suppose that this is not as bad as it could be. How long have you been working on this piece?'

Her icy voice has always made me fearful, but this time there is an almost sinister tone to it as well. I swallow hard and open my mouth to speak but nothing comes out.

'Come along girl, answer the question! When did you start work on this?'

Again I open my mouth, but still I am unable to speak.

'You insolent child, I can't waste anymore of my time with you! Get back to your seat, and you will not leave it again until this is complete to my satisfaction.'

Relief floods through me, I race away from her glare. A little fearful of how long she will keep me trapped here, I return to my seat and begin to stitch.

The Diary of Miss Ruby March

1 October 1876

The first time I ever set foot at Valley Manor, I could sense it was going to be a special place. The large house with every room decorated to a different theme wasn't just warm and welcoming, it was also intriguing, but most of all it was a friendly happy home. Yes, I knew instantly that I could be happy here.

Then I saw the gardens. Oh, how they took my breath away. They were not at all the usual formal, regimented type that I had seen before surrounding houses as grand as this one is. No, they were full of separate little havens, each one containing something to inspire and intrigue.

I have been here a whole month now, and it is hard to believe that this has not always been my home. My duties as a lady's maid to the youngest Miss Haskell, far from being hard and arduous, are proving to be pure pleasure. In fact, I am treated far more like her companion than her servant. We have already become firm friends, and this seems to be welcomed by my employer rather than anger him. However, every chance I get I lose myself in the magnificent gardens, determined to find and know every inch of them before the weather prevents me from exploring them. I have already been told that winter is harsher here than anywhere else, with snow that lasts several weeks, if not months, so I am making the most of the time I have.

I have always loved the colours of autumn, but up here they are even more spectacular than any I have seen before. The richness of reds, golds, yellows, browns and bronzes that surround me are truly breathtaking. Round every corner, through every gateway, a different scene, even more beautiful and pleasing. Each scene fills me with such serenity and joy, the likes of which I have never known before.

Today as I make my way to what has become my favourite secluded place, a small round white painted table and matching chairs, I become suddenly aware that I am not alone. I have often heard talk of 'The Dragon and The Maiden' since my arrival here, although, as yet I have not seen them for myself. When I've mentioned this to others, they have seemed shocked.

'You must have seen them. If you walk through the woods as often as you say you do? You simply can't miss them.'

But miss them I have, or at least I have seen them without seeing them if you know what I mean. However, today, as I descend the steps from the walled garden the woods feel different, as if waking from an enchanted sleep that has lasted many years which is now heralding a change. There is an unsettled, yet not fearful feeling about the place. I stop as I reach the bottom step, not only to admire another breathtaking view, but because I get the feeling that I am being watched, but from where, and by whom? To begin with I can see no-one, and then almost within touching distance, I see it. The biggest, saddest-looking bright yellow eye you can ever imagine. It seems to be looking straight at me, and yet I appear to be completely invisible to it. As I look more closely, I can begin to make out the form of a large green dragon lying exactly where there had only ever been bushes. But now, as I look more closely, I begin to believe that this great beast must have been here all along, and has indeed been sleeping.

So, this must be the dragon, but where is the maiden? Then, before I can move, it is there all around me. The deepest and most melancholic sigh I have ever heard. Surely it must be coming from the dragon? But no, the mossy mound I have walked past so often is moving with only the smallest rustle through the carpet of leaves on the ground. I stand motionless and silent; I recall a picture hanging in my room. Its title, 'A Maiden loves' now becomes real as the dragon and the maiden replay the scene in front of me. Has anyone ever witnessed this before? Is this what people have tried to tell me about?

I continue to watch as the most beautifully touching scene unfolds. The moss maiden appears from between the solemnly bowing trees, and the mournful dragon moves closer to her, the dragon's tail wraps itself tenderly around the maiden as she appears to lay herself beside the dragon, resting her head upon his huge clawed feet. Then, one giant teardrop falls from the great yellow eye, before everything suddenly stills and returns to normal. The dragon is once more sleeping, or is it in fact just a series of bushes after all? The moss maiden is once again in her usual position a few feet behind me, concealed by the thick low undergrowth. Did I really see what I saw? Or is my over-imaginative mind simply playing tricks on me?

I finally continue my journey towards the small hidden area where I often sit, but today, instead of continuing to write in my old diary, I know I have to begin writing a new one.

In this new diary I decide to tell the story of what I have witnessed this morning, and on my return to the house, I will try and find out as much as I can from the others that live here about the dragon and the maiden. Someone must know the truth, or if not, it has to be recorded somewhere. In the enormous library which exists here, there must be some information about such a strange, but powerful occurrence. I begin to write, and the words flow so easily that by the time I look up from the paper again the entire scene has changed from a bright autumn day, to a lowering grey sinister one. This is now accompanied by a distinct chill in the air. I decide to return to the house and continue my work there.

As I return along the same path I had taken only a short while ago, I realise that the chill is increasing at an alarming rate with the ever-darkening sky. Perhaps today's events signal the beginning of the long harsh winter I've been told about? As soon as I arrive back at the Manor there is a definite difference in the atmosphere. I head straight to my room to study the picture 'A Maiden Loves' more closely. I make my way immediately up the stairs, only to find my door standing open. I hesitate a short distance away, unsure whether it is safe for me to enter; this strange atmosphere makes me feel uncertain. But I can hear nothing, so I decide to go in anyway. After all, it is my room. As I hope no-one is inside, I walk in; the picture is still hanging above the fireplace. I lift it down and carry it carefully to the bed, but just as I am about to place the picture on the foot of the bed, a small folded piece of paper catches my attention. Carefully placed on my pillow, possibly by the same person who left my door open. Unfolding it, I read the following short, yet intriguing message.

I know what you have seen,
Because I have seen it too,
Meet me at six in the room of green,
For I have a tale to tell you.

I stand amazed, how could anyone know what I had seen? I had been quite alone this morning, and I know I could not have been seen from the house. Pushing this thought to one side knowing that this meeting will be my best chance to find out the truth, I glance at the wall clock visible in the hall, it is already 3pm. I decide to make my way to the library. Armed with my book, pen and picture I leave my room. I will be ready and fully equipped to write down the story I will hear. I am now so excited about my new project that I cannot wait to continue with it.

As the afternoon draws on however, and I discover more and more, I cannot help wondering whether perhaps once it is written, it may be better to keep this tale hidden away so that the secrets of the past can remain just that. This apparently tragic secret mystery, only intended to be witnessed by the chosen few, for I now firmly believe that today's events were a privilege, not a right, and should not be made public at all.

The Diary of Miss Ruby March

11 January 1877

The icy chill of winter is even more emphasized this morning, with the grass encrusted with white crystals causing a crunch beneath my boots, and the mist swirling around me. A watery sun fights hard to warm the frozen earth, unsuccessfully trying to melt the sparkling frost. The ancient stone-built bridge, with its weathered appearance, seems to hold an even greater mystery. It almost looks suspended in its state of timeless. The dark skeletonic shapes of the leafless, dormant trees only enforce the impression of somewhere that has long since been abandoned. Yet, there is something else, the source of which I cannot yet fathom, but it is causing me to believe that this long, enforced sleep of winter may soon be coming to an end.

Since my arrival here only four months ago, so much about me has changed. I have both seen and experienced things which once I would never have thought possible, and this morning I cannot shake the feeling that today could well turn out to be another special one. Perhaps even the most special yet. The gardens and house are continually revealing their secrets, but recently I have begun walking a little further from their confines. It was on one of these expeditions, that I discovered the stream and the area I now find myself drawn to on a fairly regular basis.

Dressed in the warmest clothes I own, I leave the house just as the dawn is beginning to break, with no clear idea where I am heading. It is only when I reach the end of the drive, I find myself being pulled towards this secluded, apparently forgotten spot. The chill and frost have penetrated my clothing long before I get here, but something is encouraging me to continue and not return to the comforting warmth of the house.

Now I am here I can feel a sense of expectation, not just inside me, but all around. Have I been called here to witness another awakening? If so, what will it be?

Drawing my cape closer around me, I find an old tree stump and sit cautiously on it, curling up as tightly as I can with my arms hugging my knees firmly, trying to salvage any tiny bit of warmth I can. This is not terribly successful, but strangely I really don't mind. I remain sitting on my stump for several minutes, and begin to doubt whether I had in fact felt anything at all. But then, just as I was about to try and get up and begin my walk home, everything begins to change.

The Diary of Miss Ruby March

A lone bird begins to sing high in the trees above my head, the water appears to be responding with its own peculiar melody, and then I see it. A sight so beautiful yet almost mournful, hot salty tears begin to trickle from my eyes. A lady with the palest, yet most perfect complexion, dressed in a gown made almost completely from the most delicate of blossoms, her elegance is unrivalled by any I have ever seen, she appears on the top of the bridge and begins to dance. Her movements are so exquisite; I am utterly captivated and almost miss the other figure rising up from the water. It is only when he reaches his hand up towards her that I see the whole scene. Her tiny porcelain-like white hand completely disappears into his much bigger, yet equally as pale one. Almost instantly the two figures become entwined over the water before finally, they seem to melt into the mist. Just as with the Dragon and the Maiden, I sit motionless, hardly able to breathe throughout this utterly captivating event, and for what seems a long while afterwards.

Why is this place choosing to reveal its most precious secrets to me? This is a question I cannot even begin to answer. Once again, I know I need to return to the house and continue my research. I try to uncurl myself, but the cold is so intense, I have become stiff all over and am barely able to stand, let alone walk. As I struggle to get up, I look all around me. Something has changed, I don't recognise where I am. When I witnessed the Dragon and the Maiden, everything had returned apparently to normal, but this time there is nothing that I recognise. Is this new awakening still not complete?

Having finally managed to stand, and get a small amount of feeling back into my ice-like body, I dare not sit back down on my stump, and besides, for the first time I begin to feel a very real sense of fear, like something is lurking ready to pounce. It is only now that I begin to hear it. At least, I think I do, although in some ways it begins as more of a vibration, and continues to build into something more audible. It is a sound almost unlike any other I have ever heard. A low haunting sound that should send a shiver down my spine, and yet, there is something almost comforting in it. Should I flee, but where would I go? Surely I am safer staying here? I feel as if I am being pulled in different directions. I find I am completely enveloped by it, and yet there appears to be nothing there. The sound has stopped building in volume now, has remained constant for the last few minutes.

Still standing, but unable to move, I begin to focus once more on the image I had seen a short while ago. What is happening here? What does all this mean? Why have I been chosen to witness these two almost unbelievable, yet powerfully moving events? I have never really belonged anywhere until now. Throughout my life I have always been considered to be insignificant, worthless, a burden.   All these thoughts begin to overwhelm me, and I am once again in tears. Years of abandonment, hurt, pain and not a little inflicted guilt, are pouring out of me all at once. Unable to stop, my knees buckle, my legs give way, and I once again huddle on the old tree stump. Why now? After all these years, why is it I can suddenly let everything out? Am I finally letting go. It makes no sense! For the first time in my fourteen years I have finally been accepted. I actually belong somewhere; I should be happy, but right at this moment, all I feel is utter misery.

By the time I am once more able to lift my head and look around me, I realise that the noise has stopped. Also, I can no longer even see the bridge, or the stream. Instead, I find myself, no longer curled up on an old tree stump, but in the middle of a flower-filled spring garden which surrounds a small, but beautiful thatched cottage. The icy chill of earlier has left me, and the still watery sun feels like it has some warmth in it. Seeing light shining out of every window, and a gentle plume of smoke rising from the chimney, I clamber rather inelegantly to my feet. Now convinced that I am completely lost, and feeling confused, if not a little scared, and seeing that there is no-one about, I decide I have no choice but to approach the cottage and knock on the door.

As I approach the door, the fragrance coming from the roses surrounding it and the porch is almost overwhelming. I stop, to take in the scent and to enjoy this enchanting place. There is a tranquillity here that I have never found or known before, and I find myself quite mesmerised by it.

I am still standing, only a few feet from the door several minutes later, when I realise that I am no longer alone, and that the door now stands open.

'Oh, please excuse me, I...I did not mean to disturb you, but I appear to be lost. I was so enchanted by your beautiful garden that I haven't yet made it to the door to ask for directions back to the Manor.'

The Diary of Miss Ruby March

'Dearest child, you need not apologise, and as for being lost, nothing could be further from the truth. We have been expecting you for a long while, won't you come in?'

Feeling confused, yet not afraid, I step inside the cottage. Who is this gentle young lady living in the cottage? What does she mean I have been expected for a long while and why did she say we? As soon as I step over the threshold I feel warm and safe again.

'Now, I am sure you have many questions you wish to ask me, Ruby.'

How does she know my name? My expression betrays my feeling of shock, as my host sits herself beside me and takes my hand in her own patting it reassuringly.

'Dearest Ruby, I am sure that your first question is connected to my identity, and how a complete stranger knows your name. Well, let me explain the second part first, as I believe this will be easier for you to understand. From the day you arrived at the Manor four months ago, I have been watching and waiting for this opportunity. It was after all, I who made the family aware of you and your suitability as a companion to the young mistress. I myself once came from that place of horror and torment, and regularly witnessed your plight as I suffered and endured my own looking on from a distance. I was eventually rescued by the family, and employed as a companion to their oldest daughter before… well, never mind that now, that sad tale is for another day, but this I hope explains how I know your name. As for whom I am, that is, I'm afraid going to have to remain a secret for a while yet as you will need to discover this truth for yourself.'

My host pauses, with a look of longing that is so melancholic, it almost makes me start crying again, but she soon appears to force herself to recover and continues. 'But as to how you found your way here, that is something I can try to explain, although it may make no sense to you at the moment.

As I have already told you, we share a connection as we have both come from the same dark place, do you remember the note you discovered on your pillow?'

I nod, hardly able to believe what I think I am about to be told.

'Well, I dearly wanted to meet that day, but decided in the end that it would be better to wait and allow you to discover more of the secrets of this place for yourself. The truth is that you needed to find your own way. So, when you arrived today, I knew the time was right for us to meet.'

The Diary of Miss Ruby March

I sit and listen, but scarcely believe any of it. I remember vividly waiting for the writer of the note to appear, and feeling desperately disappointed, and not a little uncertain when they did not. But I had just assumed that they were unable to come or even that Miss Florence had been having a joke on me, not that they had chosen not too. I don't know whether to feel relieved or hurt, but I am far to intrigued to put my feelings into words.

'To leave the Manor on an icy mid-January morning with snow on the ground, and a biting frost-chilled wind blowing, swirling the mist at your feet, before witnessing the images you have is one thing. But, to then find yourself, somehow in a completely different place, experiencing an entirely different season would seem unbelievable to some people, but you seem to accept it. Of course you have questions, and that is only natural, but far from fleeing from my garden, you are immediately at home there. This is because you and I share more than our past experiences, and both of us have, and still do use our imagination to enable us to cope. We are just two of a privileged number to be granted such experiences as you are having, and they are given so that we can learn from them and tell the untold stories. No-one's experiences are ever exactly the same as anyone else, but all stem and grow from the same sources. This is how you have found yourself here today.'

'But…but how do I return to the Manor, and reverse the season's so I will not be missed?'

'Time here is different to that at the Manor, so you will be able to return without them knowing you have been away. Hence, the seasons will be as they were and are. As for how you return, that is quite simple. You will exit through the door and your path back will be made clear. You may leave whenever you are ready, but before you do, I must tell you that as soon as you leave here today, time will return to that at the Manor and you must not look back, for what you see will not be where we are now, and will only fill you with fear.

'But how will I come back here, for I will want to return, I know I will?'

'And you shall Ruby, when the time is right and you need to, it will happen. Just keep believing and remember this;

Reality becomes a dream,
When the dream becomes reality,
A breath of wind,

The Diary of Miss Ruby March

Can merge the two,
For people like you,
The chosen few,
Who can see across the divide,
And be part of each parallel.
So take a step,
And don't look back,
Forward you must move,
Towards a brighter future,
Where dreams for you come true.

Now, take this with you and when you are ready, open the door and walk through it.'
As I take the card in my hand I can see that it has the same words written on it as I have just heard. I feel fearful once more.

'Do you mean…do I have to leave now?'

'That is your choice, my time with you is at an end for today, but you may stay until you feel ready. Until we meet again Ruby.'

I turn my head to look at the door for only a second, but when I turn my gaze back, my host has gone. Seeing no reason to remain longer and still uncertain, I stand once more feel stronger, but why? What is it about this cottage that makes me feel so at home? I glance round once more and make my way to the door. I take hold of the handle and turn it, the door swings open easily, and I step out into the garden.

Almost instantly the summer scene which surrounds me appears to be swallowed up by winter's cruel grip, and very soon I find myself once more beside the stream, looking towards the little stone-built bridge. It is only now that the icy, winter chill begins wrapping its frosty tendrils around me as before. I am just about to turn around, when words, as if from a dream, come into my mind;

'Do not look back, for what you see will only bring you fear. It will not make sense and will cloud your vision. Be safe my dear.'

What it means I am not quite sure, but I do know it must be heeded. It is not so much a feeling, as a gentle, reassuring voice, strangely familiar, yet distant that I am aware of. So, seeing the familiar path back towards the Manor clearly ahead of me now, I begin retracing my steps, making my journey back.

The Diary of Miss Ruby March

18 February 1877

It is now the middle of February and this winter weather continues to get worse. I still try to walk somewhere each day, but the snow is so thick now that to leave the grounds is not just foolish, but impossible. The gardens that were so beautiful when I arrived, dressed in their jewel coloured autumn costumes now lay beneath a thick white blanket encrusted with sparkling crystals. Even the apparently lifeless, skeletonic trees are bejewelled with crystals. The fountain stopped flowing months ago, but the water is still there, hanging in almost suspended animation, frozen hard into great, pointed, glass-like shards of ice. I have been told by Miss Florence they are called icicles, but a name like that just doesn't feel as though it gives their beauty and apparent power enough majesty. I much prefer to think of them as nature's chandeliers.

This morning I wake to bright winter sunshine streaming through my window. Feeling encouraged and hopeful of being able to venture out for a walk today, I throw back the bed clothes and nearly leap from the warmth of my cocoon. However, almost as soon as I leave my bed, I can feel my skin tighten as the icy temperature penetrates my thin cotton nightdress, and the temptation to return to the warmth of a few moments ago is almost too great to resist. But, I persist with my endeavour, and am soon clothed as warmly as I can be, ready to discover today's blessings. All my days here have been filled with blessings of one sort or another, but today I get the feeling that perhaps I may witness another incredible awakening.

I creep downstairs and out of the house almost silently so the rest of the household are not disturbed. I take particular care not to wake my young mistress, as she has started to ask if she may accompany me on my walks. I enjoy her company, I really do, but these few times I have to myself are special to me, allowing me to escape and explore, besides, I have the feeling that she should not come today especially. I cannot explain why I feel like this, but it is almost like a warning that her presence could bring danger to both of us. This feeling causes me to leave with slightly more trepidation than usual, yet I know now something special awaits me just around the corner. Perhaps the most special awakening yet.

I have no real idea of where I am going as I have learnt now to let my feet lead me, but I soon find myself heading towards the woods and the scene of my first experiences of the awakenings I am continuing to see. Will the dragon and the maiden appear to me again, and what about the water people? As I make my way through the walled garden, towards the wooden door leading down into the woods, I begin to doubt the wisdom of entering such a place in this weather. In fact, I reach the door and pause for several minutes before opening it; I pause again, wavering before passing through it.

The urge to continue intensifies, and I find myself cautiously making my way down the steps and into the woods. I am surprised to find that the snow in here is not nearly as deep. Of course, I realise, that the thick canopy of the evergreen trees is harder for the snow to penetrate. Feeling slightly relieved by this, I am enjoying the protection of the trees from the biting cold. I feel there is almost a warmth between them, as I continue along the footpath with a renewed encouragement and enthusiasm.

I go beyond where I saw the awakening of the dragon and the maiden, past the clearing, deeper into the trees, they are so much denser here, the dappled light is only evident in much smaller patches about me. There a little log cabin is situated slightly above the path, nestled neatly among the trees and shrubs surrounding me. I have often seen this little place before, but today there is something different about it, something sombre, yet peaceful. I make my way to the window half-obscured by snow, and the remains of tall flowering stems, long since dead. I peer in expecting to find it in darkness and empty, instead, there is a dim light. A single candle flickers revealing a shadowy figure, sitting huddled in a threadbare blanket, head turned towards the door, as if in expectation of a visitor. Feeling as though I am intruding, I take a step backwards and gasp as a frozen twig snaps loudly beneath my foot. I freeze, but the figure appears not to have heard. Unsure what to do now, I carefully make my way round to the back of the cabin, then to the other side, but there are no other windows. So, I Return to the front of the cabin, the small wooden door that was closed, now stands open, and the figure appears in the doorway. I am standing in front of the figure, yet cannot see them clearly, and apparently, they cannot see me. As we stand in silence I wait, expecting to see, hear or even feel something, but no. In fact the air is so still, and atmosphere so tense, I can barely breathe.

Several minutes pass as everything appears to just hang in a suspended state. Waiting, but for what I wonder? For whom? For how long? It is not so much in expectancy, but in hope, or more accurately, in an anguished desperate hope. All the while the only thing moving appears to be the dappling of sun through the thick canopy onto the untouched crystal white blanket beneath. Then, almost imperceptibly at first, the canopy above begins to move, yet there is no sound, none at all. Even the birds appear to be hushed into a respectful silence. The movement increases and appears to resemble that of a gale, but still there is no wind and no sound. Fearing the snow that is lying on the top of the canopy may fall onto me, I look for shelter. The only place appears to be the little cabin. I search in desperation for an alternative, but can see none. I turn to look towards the cabin; the figure still stands in the doorway.

With an ever-quickening heartbeat, I move closer. As I approach the figure becomes clearer. It is a young girl, not much older than myself and exquisitely beautiful. She appears to acknowledge my presence, as she obligingly steps to one side allowing me entrance to the safety of the cabin. I am uncertain whether she sees me or merely senses me at this point. After a few seconds, she also steps inside and closes the door. It is only now in the dim light of the candle, that I see it, her almost identical appearance to that of the young mistress. I wonder why she does she not speak? Who is this strange, almost haunted-looking girl? My questions today are to remain unanswered, at least for the moment, as having just turned to glance out of the window for a second, I now find myself quite alone. Should I stay here longer? Has the canopy above once again become still? I make my way to the door and turn the handle. I panic a little, it appears to be stuck, or no, it can't be locked? The dappled winter sunlight is still visible through the small window, but now the shadows are almost dancing. This seems far more tragic and hopeless than the awakenings I have already seen. I remember the lady in the cottage referring briefly to an older daughter, a tragedy she had said. Is this the girl I have just seen? My blood is like ice in my veins, as the thought of what I may be about to witness floods into my mind. I find myself pleading, but with who?

'Please, please don't make me see anymore, I don't want to know, someone please make it stop.'

I glance out of the window once more and as suddenly as the girl has left me, the shadows and canopy are still again. I make my way to the door, again I turn the handle. This time to my surprise and great relief, the door swings back easily and I am able to exit the cabin. Everything around me appears to be the same, and yet the atmosphere still feels so different. Perhaps this awakening has only just begun. Fear grips me once more, and yet the atmosphere does not feel so much melancholic now, more reflective instead. I take a step out of the cabin and turn to close the door. I cannot. The figure of the young girl is once again standing there. I plead with her to speak.

'Please, won't you tell me who you are? I want to help you but I don't know how?'

She says nothing, but tears begin to fall from her eyes, and I can feel a deep longing to discover more about this tragic, and I fear, dark secret. I did not want to witness this part of the awakening, but for the first time, knew I would be prepared to if the need was there. I continue to watch as the forlorn, waif-like figure retreats back into the safety of the cabin closing the door behind her. Suddenly I realise the sun has disappeared and with the oppressive dimness I can only assume the whole sky is covered with heavy grey clouds. I know that this can only mean one thing. More snow.

I make my way, back past the sleeping maiden and the dragon, before finally reaching the steps leading up to the wooden door into the walled garden.

Snow is falling heavily now, and my small climb up to the door is harder than I expect. I knew I had left it open, but now it is closed to me. I push it hard, hoping that the depth of snow is not too great to prevent it from opening. It is stiff, and obviously inhibited by the snow, but I succeed in opening it just enough to squeeze through. As I enter the walled garden and leave the woods behind, my thoughts are still with the girl I have just seen. But I know I cannot ask anyone at the house about her, what if she really is the older sister of the young mistress? There is only one person who can help me, and I have no knowledge of where or even how to find her.

Just inside the door to this garden is a vine-covered, secluded seating area. I know I really should continue back to the Manor, especially with the snow falling like this, but I have always been intrigued by this place, and something is pulling me into its shelter. I enter, and although there is no way of shutting out the weather, I feel a safety and strange warmth as I sit on the bench against the back wall. I am feeling tired now, my limbs aching because of the intense cold. My fingers and toes are numb and my face stings; but as I sit here, huddled in my cape, I begin to feel as though something is soothing me from a distance. Not only do I begin to feel relaxed, but I can feel my eyes becoming heavy, and my need for sleep becomes intense.

Just a few more minutes, I think to myself, and then I must return. But, sleep overtakes me and soon I am oblivious to the snow and the cold. However, I think it is not too long before I wake with a start, and sit myself up, only to see the walled garden melt in front of me. What is happening? I begin to feel the whole secluded place rotate; will I find myself back in the woods? I shudder. What is this place? I do not have to wait long, for there in front of me is a gate, already standing open, giving me entrance to a rose-covered path. Where am I now? Where does this lead? Then, with a tremor of hope, I realise the snow has gone, and the air is fragrance-filled and warm. Could I really be back, back at her cottage? Could this be a back way? I wonder, is that why it looks so different? Am I approaching from a different entrance? A back way perhaps?

I begin to walk along the footpath, but no matter how far I travel it just seems to stretch further into the distance, or am I just not moving? I turn my head to look behind, no, I am definitely moving, as the gate I entered through is now out of sight. I also appear to be climbing a hill, as behind me the path is dropping away. Could it still be the back way to the cottage? If it is, why would such a small cottage have such a grand pathway leading to its back entrance especially when its front entrance is so homely and friendly?

Onwards I walk, now the pathway is changing, it finally appears to be opening out into something more like a driveway. This seems even stranger to me, why would a tiny cottage have the need for a driveway? I stop, unable to move. The building standing before me is most certainly not a cottage. Its ornate pillared entrance is like that of a grand palace. Where am I? What is this place? Everywhere is shut up, and there are no signs of life anywhere. As I get nearer I can also see signs of a vicious fire, this place is no more than a ruin, yet the gardens are still immaculate. My hopes of returning to the cottage feel lost in the face of this odd ruin.

I look all around me, hoping to just see some movement, something that would show me I am not alone in this once grand place. Again I question why the gardens remain so well kept, when such a magnificent house is being allowed to decay and crumble. Trying to cheer myself with the knowledge that at least here, in this place, I can enjoy the warmth and fragrance of spring, so I decide to try and take a closer look at the house. Approaching the once great door slowly, as with each step I take, the fear inside me builds. To my surprise, although there are obvious signs of damage from the fire, like the rest of the building, the door is still solid and still firmly locked from the inside. Admittance to this place seems impossible. Every window is shuttered and barred, and both doors are firmly remaining in place.

I am standing now in the rear garden, and this is as beautifully manicured and cared for as the one I had entered through. This is indeed a lonely place. Why am I being shown this? Why do I need to see a house of such obvious loss surrounded by a garden of such apparent hope? I cannot fathom the reasons behind this part of the awakening at all, yet I am convinced this is in someway connected to the events I have already witnessed this morning.

I turn and make my way back, retracing my steps, as by now I am certain to have been missed from the Manor. I consider the possibility that time here, as it is at the cottage, is not bound by that of the Manor at all? This thought urges me to stay a while longer. I make my way across the lush lawn, which looks freshly trimmed, and sit for a while on a swing seat in the lea of a large tree. As I sit swinging and enjoying the pleasant outlook, I see it, a small blue ribbon fluttering gently each time I swing, attached to it is a small piece of paper tied to the frame of this ornate, yet surprisingly comfortable, piece of garden furniture.

Untying the ribbon carefully, and unfolding the paper, I begin to read;

Dear Ruby,

I am sorry I cannot meet you in person today, but if you have made it this far you are probably feeling confused and anxious. This is only natural, but all that you have seen today will begin to become clear when you return to the Manor, and in the days that follow. You will need to visit here again and on your next visit you will

gain entrance to the hall. Now, to get back, read
the poem and follow it.
   Until we meet again.

  The way you came is not your way back,
   Look for the door without any black.
  Tie the blue ribbon around the handle,
  It will open a passageway lit by a candle.
   Follow this path as far as it goes,
And the chill winter frost will not nip at your toes.
When you think you have reached as far as it goes,
Take one more step to the room where love glows.
   You will know it at once,
   No time will have past,
  You'll be back at the Manor House,
   As unheard as a mouse.

What does this mean? I have found only two
doors, both blackened and burnt and barring
my way I ponder. Then, as if my thoughts
had conjured it up, a small white door, in the
wall, facing me. I am sure it was not there
when I looked before, but knowing my lady
from the cottage, it will not lead me wrong, as
I am sure now that she is more than just a
guide, she is my friend.

  I follow every instruction, and very soon
find myself standing back in my own room,
only seconds after leaving it. I turn to try and

go back, but alas, the passageway is no longer there. I decide that my mission now is to discover the meaning behind everything which has appeared today, beginning with the identity of the young girl in the cabin. But first my duties toward my young mistress must be attended too.

The Diary of Miss Ruby March

30 March 1877

Winter finally seems to be weakening its grip. The snow is melting and trees are waking from their frozen sleep. Buds are breaking and even the birdsong appears to be taking on a different, brighter melody. My young mistress has begun waking earlier to try and follow me on my early morning walks, and only yesterday she had beaten me to the door. Seeing I had no choice but to allow her to accompany me, I insisted we speak to her parents upon our return. She found this suggestion most disagreeable as she feared they would 'spoil her fun'. This fear proved to be unfounded though, as both her mother and father seemed delighted that she wanted to join me. However, I got the feeling that they wanted to tell me something, but at the last moment stopped themselves. It was not anything they had said, but a look which had passed between them, it said more than words ever could. It was as if they knew something and wanted to pass that knowledge on. I feared they were afraid to say, or perhaps were not allowed too? Why this would be true I didn't know, but that look remains hauntingly in my mind.

This morning I wake and know I must go

out alone, but how? What reason can I give? I ready myself quickly, and with as little sound as possible, before leaving my room. I make my way quickly downstairs and to the door, relieved to see no sign of my young mistress. I turn the key as quietly as I can, but it still seems to make the loudest clunking noise I have ever heard. The sounds seems to echo throughout every part of the Manor, I stand silent and still, waiting, hardly daring to breathe, but after a few minutes, decide I am safe to open the door and make my exit.

As I step outside closing the door behind me, I cannot help feeling a little guilty about the young mistress; after all I am employed to be her maidservant and companion. I also know when feeling as I do this morning, it is important for me to be alone. With the Manor out of sight behind the wall of the garden, my feeling of guilt is replaced by another more dominant sensation of uncertainty or is it distrustfulness? I feel as though I am not alone any longer. Is someone following me? Who is it? Why don't they make themselves known?

Then a new thought hits me, could the young mistress be following out of sight? This could be a real problem; she could endanger both of us. Stopping at the door to the woods, I wait but do not turn round straight away. There is nowhere in here to hide, apart from the secluded seating place, but standing where I am, it is quite obvious there is nobody in there. Looking all around me and seeing no-one, I decide to continue, although I still feel a presence with me.

I find myself very quickly being drawn towards the woods. Part of me had wanted to turn and go the other way as I did not know if I wanted to go back to the scene of the last awakening, as it had been so sad. However, my curiosity soon took over and now I am once again making my way through the woods. Passing the dragon and the maiden, heading towards the clearing with its table and chairs, I stop abruptly facing a very large tree. It is obviously many years old, and appears to have three separate trunks growing out of the same route system. It is not this however that makes me stop, but what I think I see disappear through the gap between two of these trunks. The sun is shining and the spring breeze is dancing lively through the trees, causing shadows to move and change in a mischievous way. I thought I saw a figure step through the gap, without emerging on the other side. It could just have been a trick of the light and dancing shadows. No, there it is again. Do they want me to follow them?

Seeing no-one else about, I move closer. Again they disappear through the gap. Feeling certain now they want me to follow them, I approach the tree. The figure has not reappeared, so before entering the gap, I pause and, holding firmly on to the trunk, attempt to peer through. To my disappointment, all I can see is a very normal view of the other side of the tree and no sign of the figure. Is it just my imagination? A cold shiver runs right through me as I remember the words once spoken to me by one of the cruellest people I had known;

'Ruby March! That imagination of yours will only get you into trouble!'
This thought stops me in my tracks. My only thoughts now are filled with fear and dread. Then I remember the last awakening I had witnessed, not beautiful like the first two, but dark and melancholic. Perhaps this cruel, hateful woman had been right? Maybe I was being punished for prying into something which had nothing to do with me. Feeling myself become weak and my eyes prick with tears, I turn and begin to walk away.

For the first time since my arrival here, almost seven months ago, I feel alone, miserable and terrified. I walk a few paces from the tree; I hear a voice calling my name. I stop. A voice filled with such love and warmth, I know it at once as the lady from the cottage.

'Ruby, Ruby, have you forgotten what I told you? You have begun to doubt and look back haven't you? Remember to always go forward and leave the past behind you. Those days of horror are past, and your life now is filled with pleasure and love. Return to the tree and take that step, for what lies beyond can only be seen when you truly trust and believe.'

Spinning round as quickly as I can, I am disappointed not to find her, but, hoping that I may find her again today, I return to the tree and step through the gap. Instantly the scene around me changes. I find myself back in the garden of the fire-damaged house, only this time, instead of being a place of sorrow and heartache, there is a feeling of joy and no sign of the vicious fire anywhere. The garden appears almost identical, but far from being a place of silence, I can now here the excited chatter and laughter of children coming from inside the house.

Is this when I am to gain access to this

house? I can't just let myself in, that wouldn't be right, yet the closer to the house I get, the stronger I feel its pull.

The great front door is now before me, standing open as if waiting for my arrival, but still I pause before stepping inside. Seeing nobody around, I make my way to the staircase and begin to climb to the room where the chattering and laughter is coming from. A door opens in front of me and out of it run two young girls of about my own age. One I recognise instantly as the figure from the cabin, but she is happy here, not like the last time I saw her. The other girl also seems strangely familiar, yet I cannot name her or identify where I have seen her before. They rush straight past without seeing me, and are down the stairs, out of the door and away before I can say anything. I should not be surprised, as in all the other awakenings I have witnessed; I have seen them without my presence without my presence being noticed before.

Do I turn and follow the girls outside, or do I explore the rest of the house? I may not get back here again and am curious to see everything. I decide to look around; keeping in mind I have been told to always move forward. I make my way to the open door from which the girls had made their exit only a few moments ago, and enter. Immediately I stop, this room…it is the exact mirror image of my own room back at the Manor. How can this be? This makes no sense, unless…no it couldn't be could it? I feel such a familiarity about the whole place, I realise now that is what I had felt before when I was in the garden. This is the Manor, but in a time past, and before the devastating fire. Why am I seeing this?

I stand still for several minutes; a new recognition floods my mind. The other girl, she was…how could it be? But it was. It was Elsie, my only friend from the unhappy years spent with my Aunt and Uncle. In fact, the only friend I had ever truly had until I came here. I cannot help feeling there should be another link with her, but I can't make it, at least not yet, or can I? If that girl is Elsie and the other girl is the older daughter, then…I gulp hard, then Elsie is the lady at the cottage, because she was her companion. Feeling giddy and emotional, I collapse into a chair. I am not crying, but cannot understand why I am being shown this, or what it all means?

I come too with a start, had I passed out? I hear a knock at the door, which is now closed. Am I somehow back in my room at the

Manor? No, this is still the room I entered, so why is the door closed and who is knocking on the door? Getting up from the chair, I realise I am no longer alone, and that Elsie is also here, but she still cannot see me, at least I don't think she can. The door opens and the older daughter enters. The scene before me now is not a happy one, but filled with sorrow and heartache, what is happening here? Our surroundings have altered too; we are no longer in the beautiful room, but standing outside watching the house engulfed by flames.

As I look beside me, it is with a sickening realisation that there are now only two of us standing there, myself and Elsie. The older daughter is nowhere to be seen. Looking at Elsie I realise that she is no longer unaware of my presence and I am once again looking at my lady from the cottage. Returning my blurred gaze towards the house, I see only the blackened shell of the Manor from before.

Pleading with her I beg Elsie to tell me the truth about all that I have seen.

'What happened here Elsie? I must know the truth.'

Her gentle sweet voice brings back a comfort known so long ago.

'You will Ruby, now come, follow me

and we will return to the cottage.'

Although feeling shocked and saddened by all that I have just witnessed, I cannot help feeling glad at the prospect of returning to the cottage where I had first met Elsie again after so many years. But why did I not recognise her last time? Why did it take such a tragedy to reunite us? None of what I have witnessed today is making any sense, but as we arrive at the cottage I at least begin to feel safe again.

The cottage has not altered at all since my first visit. The garden also appears to have stood still, but how? Everything at the Manor has changed so much. I can remember Elsie saying that time here is different, but to not move on at all does not make sense. We enter the cottage and I take a seat at the table as before. It is only now that I realise I don't have any knowledge of how we came to find ourselves here. I don't even remember leaving the scene of the fire, or passing anything recognisable as we made our way here. It is almost as if we simply turned round where we stood and the cottage appeared.

'Ruby, are you alright child? I understand that today has been confusing and upsetting, but it was necessary for you to see it before I can even begin to explain any of what you have seen recently, or you would understand none of it.'

I do not speak but listen intently as she begins to tell me a story so filled with heartache and sorrow that tears fall freely within seconds, but not before explaining one of my many questions.

'Ruby, I am sure you are curious as to why you did not recognise me before? Sometimes we are prevented from seeing things for a reason. If you had known me before you would have wanted to cling to what we had when you were very young. This cannot happen, and you don't need me that way anymore. There is something else you will need to know about me, but you will only discover this truth when you are stronger.

Do you remember the first day you arrived at the cottage and I told you that the sad tale about the oldest daughter was for another time? Well that time is now. All that you have seen during the last two awakenings which you have witnessed is only part of this tragic story. But, I must tell you now the tragedy may not be what you expect. There was indeed a vicious fire as you have seen, and we stood watching I could see you were aware that Miss Charlotte was not with us. I am sure you assumed that she perished in the fire, but this is not true. She still lives to this day. Her parents never did blame her, if anything they blamed themselves, but it was really just a tragic accident no-one could have foreseen.'

'Elsie please, tell me, if Miss Charlotte did not perish, where is she now?'

'All in good time Ruby, but first I must explain about the day of the fire a little more. It was a day much like today when winter had all but ended, and spring was waking everything from a state of dormant slumber to a time of growth and abundance. A fire still crackled in the hearth as it was cold in the Manor and young Master Edward was fascinated by the flames. He had never gone too close or put anything into the fire, but that fateful day this changed and his curiosity must have overwhelmed him. He had been out walking in the gardens with his sister and myself, but without our knowledge had returned to the house before us. By the time we realised he was no longer with us it was too late. We immediately quickened our pace and returned to the Manor, only to find it already well alight, flames jumping from every window, and with an oppressive sickness deep inside us, we could only guess at what had happened.

The damage to the Manor was severe, and although Master Edward's tiny body was never found, it was assumed he had perished in the blaze. He has certainly never been seen since, and Miss Charlotte refused to be comforted and eventually took herself away from the Manor, her family and me. Nobody knew where she had gone or even if she was alive, she was so young at just fifteen years of age. Poor Lord and Lady Haskell, already grieving at the devastating loss of one child never believed they could be happy again, that is until Miss Florence was born nearly fifteen years ago. I knew that I could not stay, but I had nowhere to go. The guilt and anguish that I felt was only intensifying the pain of my Master and Mistress, and despite their pleading with me to stay, telling me that my presence was a comfort to them because, 'at least we could give you a better life' they said. But I knew I had to return to London. I had relatives there, although I had never met them, felt as though I had no choice. I left that same day vowing never to return, but circumstances once again proved to determine yet another twist in this tale. It was however, while I was away that…'

Elsie pauses.

The Diary of Miss Ruby March

'Why have you stopped Elsie? Please, won't you finish what you were going to say?' A look of almost haunted melancholy fleetingly grips my most treasured friend, but she soon forces herself to smile, and changing the subject, returns to the story of Miss Charlotte.

'Not now Ruby, one day you will understand why. But you asked me earlier about Miss Charlotte did you not? Well, it must have been about three years after I had left the Manor behind me; a letter arrived with my name on the envelope. I recognised in an instant the hand in which it was written, my one glimmer of hope in an existence which had now become almost unbearable apart from… But you know all about that life.'

She smiles sadly at me then continues.

'It was from Miss Charlotte herself, but how she had found me in that terrible place, I could not begin to imagine. But, found me she had, was my life about to change again? But how could I go back? How could I leave…? With my heart racing and fingers trembling, I opened the envelope, and with tears burning to be allowed to fall, read the words contained within it.

It told a tale of such sorrow and torment

that you need not hear, at least not now, but it finished by saying that she had returned to the Manor and although she could no longer face living there, she had persuaded her parents to let her have the gatehouse cottage. They had only allowed this after she had told them she was going to find me and bring me back also. That cottage my dearest Ruby is where we find ourselves now.'

'But where is Miss Charlotte, and why do I only ever see her as a child?'

'These questions are for another day child, but you must promise me one thing.'

'Of course Elsie, anything.'

'You say that now, but when you hear what it is that I am asking of you, you may not find it so easy to agree.'

I listen intently to what she says, my head already spinning and so full of unanswered questions, I very much doubt whether this latest request can be that difficult to obey.

'While you have been at the Manor, have you ever discovered the spiral staircase and the locked room at the top of it?'

'Why yes, Miss Florence and I talk of it often and really enjoy making up stories about it. I did ask her once where the key was, but she told me she has no memory of a key ever being there, or anyone visiting it.

Although, she did admit that she was curious about why it was always locked. She even asked her parents about it, but they just told her the key was lost many years ago, and that there was nothing up there apart from the 'Turret Room' which was no longer used or needed.'

'Ruby, please promise me that whatever you do, and however curious you two become, you will never try and enter that place?'

Her tone and the look on her face become more solemn and serious than I have ever seen before, that I agree instantly.

'I need to hear you say it, please promise me Ruby, and never, ever ask me why.'

Elsie is almost in tears, and visibly shaken by the thought of the place.

'I do promise Elsie, I would never do anything to hurt or upset you.'

'Dearest Ruby I ask this not for myself, but for you. Whatever you think you may hear or see, never go back on that promise. There may come a time when the secrets held in there need to be revealed, but until then please stay away.'

'I will Elsie, I promise.'

With a brighter tone returning to her voice

and something more like her usual tenderly caring expression, she says something I had been waiting to hear but hoping not to.

'Now Ruby, it is time for you to be getting back to the Manor and Miss Florence. As before, when you open the door don't look back, just move forward and you will be back in no time at all.

'Must I go right now? Can I not stay just a little longer?'

'I would love you to, but as I have already told you, time here is different to time at the Manor, so for now at least our times together must be limited. We will be together again soon, I promise, and maybe one day things will be different.'

With a fond embrace we part company again, and I return to the Manor. This time Miss Florence meets me on the steps before I can enter and berates me for leaving without her this morning. As we enter together, I cannot help wondering if Miss Florence even knows of her brother and sister? I also feel she cannot know how lucky she is not to have seen and heard all that I have. But I also know how lucky I am to have been granted the privilege of seeing and hearing them.

The Diary of Miss Ruby March

17 April 1877

Spring is really beginning to take over, and winter seems almost like a dream, it is only on the tops of the hills that there is any snow, and there are carpets of flowers everywhere. It is becoming increasingly difficult to escape from the Manor alone in the mornings now, Miss Florence is usually ready several minutes ahead of me and waiting outside my door.

However, this morning the intensity of the dawn chorus wakens me far earlier than usual, and I am able to escape before anyone else is up. I leave just as the sun appears on the horizon, and the cacophony which surrounds me lifts my spirit so much, that I feel as though I am dancing through the gardens rather than walking. It is only after a few minutes that I realise I am in fact skipping, and as the sun rises further into the sky, I just know today is going to be another really special one.

I have not journeyed as far as I usually do, when something makes me stop. I find myself standing next to the sundial. I have of course noticed this before, but for many weeks it had been covered with snow, so I had simply walked past it. But, this morning the bright spring sunshine is casting shadows upon it, the likes of which I have never seen. I know of course that you are supposed to be able to tell the time by it, although I wouldn't be able too. But, the shadows on it now are certainly not right for this purpose. They appear to be dancing joyfully, and somehow, I feel they want me to join them. How can I? Moving closer I can sense the ground begin to turn, everything is spinning and whirling so fast around me, but the sundial appears not to be moving at all, in fact it is quite still.

I place my hands upon it to steady myself and instantly everything stops. Looking around me, to begin with my vision is blurred so nothing appears to have changed, but as I continue to look around me, I begin to see that everything has changed. I am in a place I have never seen before. The air is filled with a fragrance so warm and sweet, I feel as though I could just curl up and fall asleep. I know however, that I must resist this temptation as the awakening has started. Just the feeling that this place gives, leads me to believe that today will be filled with hope and joy, but also that I may discover a truth almost unbelievable.

I begin to move away from the sundial towards a lush green lawn surrounded by the most wonderful trees and blooms my eyes have ever been blessed by. It is only now that I hear it, distantly at first, but yes, definitely getting closer; a voice, but not just any voice, the sweetest purest voice my ears have ever been filled with, and singing the most beautiful melody. I stop moving and just listen; as if it is entrancing me. It is not the voice of dearest Elsie, or even that of Miss Charlotte. No it is the voice of a young child, it sounds like they are simply expressing pure joy at what they are seeing, hearing, feeling and living. I cannot see who this child is, but something tells me that I have already heard about them, or know of them during a previous awakening.

I begin to move towards the voice once more, and as I turn the next corner, I see the child from whence the sound comes. A young boy of about three or four, cheerfully running and jumping around the skirts of a very young, but beautiful lady. I recognise her instantly as the Mistress from the Manor and the mother of Miss Florence. The scene I am seeing must have taken place at least sixteen years earlier, but if that is the case, she must be much older than she appears to be. How can this be the same person? The longer I stand here, the more the scene enchants me.

Not only by the sweet little child, who by now I assume is Master Edward, but by the entire scene and place. Master Edward, I can only describe as delightful. His tight blonde curls bounce playfully on his head as he bounces in the same manner around his mother. His chubby, cheerful, cheeky little face with its rosy cheeks and piercing blue eyes would not fail to captivate the heart of anyone who saw him.

My vision becomes blurred and I am fully aware that by now my own eyes and cheeks are glistening with tears. I can only imagine the heartache and sorrow that was felt by all who knew and loved this adorable little boy. As I continue to stand and watch this delightful tableau play out in front of me, I become aware that I am not alone; there is another person slightly to my left, standing watching at a slightly greater distance than myself. I turn expecting to see Elsie, but instead I catch the most fleeting glimpse of a young lady, closely resembling Miss Charlotte. I cannot be certain, as she disappears so quickly, but if it is her, that means she still lives nearby. It also means that, like Elsie and myself, she is able to see the awakenings. Does this mean that Miss Florence can also see them? What would happen if…?

My thoughts are interrupted at this point by a change in the air. I am unable to explain it, but something is different.

I turn back towards the tableau, only to discover a very different scene. This one breaks my heart. There is the mistress again, only this time she is alone and sobbing bitterly. The Master is walking towards her and tenderly places a comforting hand on her shoulder. She turns towards him burying her head in her husband's embrace, as he in turn begins to sob too. I turn away. I feel as though I am intruding on this most intimate grief-stricken moment. As I turn I hear Elsie's voice calling to me;

Do not turn away dear Ruby,
This is something you must see,
Do not let your heart break,
Or this one scene your joy take,
Keep watching child and you will know,
Even as your own tears flow,
How many blessings life can bring,
And that one day soon again you'll sing.
When this scene comes to an end,
Follow the path around the next bend,
There you will find an answer you seek,
Before you and I can once again speak.

I return my gaze to heart-wrenching scene. The Mistress can be clearly seen still, only this time there is a new child bouncing around her skirts. I stand, hardly believing what I am seeing. This child is Miss Florence, and her mother is smiling once more. Then I hear it, the same sweet song which had called me here to begin with, only this time it is the Mistress herself singing it. I continue to watch; the mistress takes Miss Florence by the hand and walks away deep in thought, but contentedly all the same. Am I to follow now, or is there more to see? I am just about to chase their steps on the same foot path, when Miss Charlotte enters the scene again, and sits just where her mother had been only a few moments earlier.

Is this part of the awakening? Does she know I am here? Her fleeting appearance a short while ago leads me to believe she does know, or perhaps she was frightened of being seen by someone else? Whether she is aware of me or not, this time she stays where she is. Does she really not see me? Or does she just not care anymore?

As I continue to watch, there is no singing now, even the birdsong seems to be strangely muted. I begin to wonder whether she comes here regularly, but where is here? Why have I not found this place before?

After a few more minutes Miss Charlotte gets up and begins coming towards me. What should I do? Perhaps I shouldn't be here after all? She passes by me apparently unseeing, and I know now that I must follow the path. The cacophony of the dawn chorus was replaced by singing; this in turn has been replaced by more bird song, but much gentler and more wistful than before. The pathway meanders beside the lawn before leading me through a pretty rose-covered walkway. I don't know what I expect to find as I pass beneath, but it certainly is not the scene that greets me as I emerge.

I find myself, standing in a formal courtyard surrounded by statues, there are fountains and a high wall with creepers growing in and covering all four corners of the stonework. The atmosphere here is different too, not exactly sinister, but certainly still and almost distant. Why have I been guided here? There is still some warmth to the air, but the sweet fragrance from the garden has gone.

I stand alone here for several minutes wondering what is about to happen? Who is about to appear? What am I even doing here? Then, I become aware of a figure coming towards me, a figure not yet known to me, but something about him is telling me to hide.

Where am I supposed to hide in here? The statues are not big enough, the fountains are too obvious, my only choice seems to be to try and conceal myself in one of the corners amongst the dense creepers. The figure is approaching me quite rapidly; am I already too late? As I try to hide myself in the nearest corner, he reaches the spot I had just been standing in. This must be still part of the awakening, isn't it? Doubt creeps into my thoughts. He stops, looking all around as though searching for something or someone, me? Maybe he had seen me after all? Or is he searching, for someone else? He takes a seat beside one of the fountains idly stirring the water with one hand while the other remains hidden beneath his cape.

I realise now how little of him I can actually see. Everything within me is telling me to make my escape while he is not looking, that I should fear this man, yet I do not. I cannot see his face clearly, yet I imagine him to be young, barely an adult and there is something about him that leads me to believe he is deeply troubled and unhappy, even tormented. The longer I observe this figure from my concealed corner, the more I find myself longing to know more, to know the truth. But how can I? How will I find out?

'Oh Elsie, where are you? Can you not help me? Tell me something about him?'
I did not mean to say this out loud, and only realise I have when he looks in my direction.

I endeavour to conceal myself further within the creeper, but soon realise my efforts in this are futile and only drawing attention to my presence. I stop moving completely, hardly daring to breathe. He soon looks away again. He must have seen me, he looked straight at me? Yet, he is still apparently unaware of my presence. Perhaps he thought it was just the wind rustling the leaves and branches, or perhaps… my heart begins to pound hard in my chest, perhaps he has known I was here all along. Perhaps he has seen me anyway as he came towards me to begin with? Is he just sitting there waiting, knowing that eventually I will have to leave my corner and that my only escape is either back the way I have come, or to keep going which will take me right past him. Immediately the feeling of fear floods into me with such power that I am sure I will not be able to move even if I see a chance. Can I really be in this much danger from someone, who until now, has appeared to have no concern about my presence? Or does he truly not know I am here?

This state of terror continues, I see him get up and move off in the direction I had just come from. Several minutes pass before I dare to move. Afraid still even though I can see from my corner he is nowhere to be seen, I remain tight against the wall and under the cover of the creeper for a long time.

Eventually I move onwards and reach a small gateway with its pretty gate standing open and am relieved to be out of that place. However, my thoughts now return to Elsie's words of earlier. She told me I would find an answer I had been seeking. That doesn't make any sense. So far I have only encountered yet more questions, and still Elsie is nowhere to be seen. I continue to follow the path and, having left the courtyard, I now find myself in a place unlike any I have visited before.

I am surrounded by, what I assume to be, hedges. They are not clipped and controlled like all the others I have seen, they are wild-looking, growing out of control. The path has all but disappeared and the sky can only be glimpsed through tangles of twigs and leaves above my head. I see no flowers here, and the deeper I go into this wilderness, the less certain I am that I should even be in this place. How can I find any answers in a wilderness like this?

I, follow what I assume is a path, taking a sharp corner, the tangle completely clears and I am back out in warm sunshine. Daring to glance quickly behind me, I can see a mass of overgrown hedges, but where I am now is beautiful. The path takes me along another rose-covered walkway and at the far end sunlight is glistening like silver and diamonds on water. I have never noticed a lake or pond here, and the only place I have seen a stream flowing is under the little bridge outside the estate grounds. As I get nearer I can see there is no stream, but a huge lake with an island at the centre. On the island is the most welcome sight of all, Elsie's little cottage, but how can I get there?

Seeing a seat at the water's edge, I make my way there and sit down looking wistfully across the water. Moments later, I hear a familiar melody, but this time the voice singing it is rich and deep with the quality of velvet. The voice is coming from behind me. I dare not turn round, as it continues to get closer. I feel myself stiffen all over, as the shadow of the owner of the voice falls by my side. I cannot help but gasp as I glance at it and recognise its shape immediately as the mysterious figure from earlier. In an attempt to protect, maybe even save myself, I blurt out an anguished plea.

'Please, please, I mean you no harm sir; I do not wish to intrude on your privacy, earlier or now, please don't hurt me.'

Even I can hear the faltering nature of my voice. The singing stops, as a hand gently grips my shoulder before it and the shadow disappear completely, or so I think when I eventually open my eyes.

Too afraid to look up, I stare into the water, I see a face looking up at me before it too vanishes. Was, it the Master Edward? So that is the answer I have been seeking? But Elsie said that he had never been seen since the fire? What is happening here?

As I look towards the water again, I see a stepping stone where the face of Master Edward had been, and as I look further across the water, Elsie appears on the island beckoning to me to go across.

But how can I, there is only one stepping stone? I suddenly recall Elsie's words, about looking forward and trusting, so I step onto the stone and another emerges in front of me. Each step forward, another stone emerges and soon Elsie and I are once again standing in the garden of her cottage.

'Come in Ruby, you have seen much today and I know you will want to talk about it, but before you do, I must first explain some things to you.'

Feeling relieved to finally be here, I step inside the cottage and take my usual seat. As I do so, I notice that there are three cups and saucers waiting on the table today instead of the usual two. But before I can say anything, Elsie acknowledges my confused perception with her usual knowing smile.

'Dearest Ruby, please do not look so concerned, we will indeed be joined by a third person today, but you need not fear or dread this meeting for you have already met them. Although, until today they will not have spoken to you despite your best efforts. But, before the time comes for them to join us, you and I need to talk. As I said when you arrived here today, before you talk about all you have seen and experienced, I have a few things which I need to explain to you, which will hopefully answer at least a few of the many questions you must have.

You will remember that last time you were here, we spoke about the fire and I told you that Master Edward had not been seen since? Well, that is only partly true. If you remember, I also told you that his tiny body was never found, but Master Edward certainly was. It was Miss Charlotte herself who found him cowering in a corner, terrified but silent and also with burns to his poor little face and one of his hands where he had tried to protect himself.'

'Well if he was alive why did Miss Charlotte not tell her parents?'

'Please Ruby be patient and let me continue, it will become clearer and our time is short. The guilt Miss Charlotte felt was immense, and the sight of her baby brother like this was almost too much for her to bear, so she decided to keep him hidden until together, they could make their escape. This is the real reason for her leaving the Manor, she has been caring for him ever since. It is indeed Master Edward you have seen today but still he does not speak, and although his scaring has faded he will only leave the protection of home if completely concealed.'

'But I heard him singing only a few minutes before I came across the water to you? I also saw a reflection before the first stepping stone appeared?'

'Dear Ruby, singing is Master Edwards only comfort, he is a soul in torment still, and the reflection you saw was of him as I child was it not?'

Thinking hard before I respond, I realise it was indeed a child's face that had looked up at me from the water.

'Oh Elsie, I wish I could help him, his voice is so beautiful and I know his parents would want to know the truth. They would not care how he looked. It is clear to see how much love they have for their son when I saw them so broken earlier.'

'Oh Ruby, I do understand how you feel, and how much you long to help, who knows you may well be the link we have all been waiting for, but his parents still believe to this day that he perished in that fire, and at least for now, must continue to do so. Do you understand Ruby?'

I am unable to speak. Unsure about how much I really do understand, I nod my head anyway.

'Now, before you ask more questions or talk about today, I need to introduce you properly to Miss Charlotte. It was indeed her you saw earlier today and she saw you, but the time was not right then for you to meet. There was so much more you needed to see.'

A small painted door that I have noticed before opens in the wall behind me, and Miss Charlotte appears.

The Diary of Miss Ruby March

'Hello Ruby, it is with relief and much pleasure that I am finally able to meet you properly. That day in the cabin all those weeks ago, I longed just to be able to tell you who I was, but it was too early and there were things you needed to see and be aware of first, just as Elsie must have told you.'

' Oh Miss Charlotte, there is so much of this that I just don't understand, including how people can be my age in one awakening and older or younger in another, or in the case of Master Edward within the same awakening? I know time works differently during these times; I just wish I could know how. But, there is one thing I would like to ask you if I may?'

'Of course child that is the purpose of my presence here today, but know this, the answer I can give may not be what you are expecting, or even one that you will fully understand.'

'Miss Charlotte, are you able to see the awakenings too, or are you just part of them when I see them?'

'That is hard to answer Ruby, because any answer I give will be both true and false at the same time, but what I can tell you is that from now on when you see me, we will be able to speak, much like you and Elsie do now.'

My confusion must be more evident in my expression than I realise because it is Elsie who speaks next.

'I think perhaps you have seen and tried to understand enough for today child. The time has come for you to return to the Manor, but our next meeting may be sooner than you think.'

'But I have so much more I need to ask of you, both of you, and more I want know. Please can I stay just a little longer?'

'Not this time Ruby, but know this, Miss Florence is not able to see the awakenings yet. The time may come when it is right for her too, but that is not now. You must continue to allow her to accompany you on your walks for most of the time, but as you have already discovered for yourself, you will know when this is not right. The next few awakenings may come closer together and throughout the next few months you will begin to discover things about your own life as well as the mysteries that exist here. This time is not to be feared but embraced, I am not saying that you will not feel frightened at times child, but the time will come when all your questions will be answered and your life can truly begin. Take care Ruby, and remember the warning I gave you last time you were here?'

'Do you mean about the turret room?'

'Yes, that is still to be obeyed, after today you may see or hear things that seem to be leading you up there, but you must not go there, not yet anyway. There is more for you to learn yet. You are not ready for the answers which are to be found in that place.'

'I understand, and I won't go there, I promise.'

Elsie opens the door to the cottage and both her and Miss Charlotte watch me safely back across the stepping stones, but as I reach the bank, the Manor appears before me and I find myself standing once more on the front lawn. Hurriedly I make my way inside, but as I do I realise that everyone else is still sleeping and no time has passed at all.

I return to my room to try and make sense of what I have seen, heard and experienced during this latest awakening, but nothing seems to make sense, and I soon find myself drifting back into sleep. I shake myself awake, and I begin to write.

The Diary of Miss Ruby March

1 May 1877

As I wake this morning to the sound of, what can only be described as, distant crying, has Elsie been right about the time of our next meeting? I get the feeling that this morning will be another special one. As Elsie warned me, the sound does appear to be coming from the turret room, but I do not follow it, instead I walk determinedly away. Is the awakening beginning before I even leave the house?

I make my way down stairs, as quietly as I can, noticing that Miss Florence is already waiting by the door for me. Now what do I do? She cannot come with me this morning. She has not seen me yet, as she is not facing the staircase, and I have not yet turned to descend the last few steps. So, taking even greater care now not to be heard, I make my way back up and along the corridor to the back of the Manor, where I begin to descend the narrow rear staircase. I can still hear the sound of crying, but at least I should be able to leave alone.

I don't usually leave the Manor this way, in fact the last time I did, it was in deep snow, so I don't really recall where I come out. The door is locked and the large key is stiff in the lock, the sound it makes, as it eventually turns, seems to echo around for ages. I freeze and wait. After several minutes with no-one appearing, I decide that it is safe to continue. The small wooden door opens surprisingly easily once unlocked and I step out-side closing it carefully behind me. It is only now I take in my surroundings. I am, back in the courtyard where I had first seen Master Edward only a few days earlier, only this time the atmosphere is different. It is not still and distant as before, but almost expectant as though a long awaited event is about to occur. The birds are singing heartily again, but this time there is almost an excitement amongst them too.

I make my way further in, and this time find myself being drawn to the far side, where I discover a small wooden door almost completely concealed by creeper. Carefully pushing the creeper's tendrils to one side I find the handle, turning it in hope rather than expectation, to my surprise the door opens. Stepping through, I find myself once more in the vicinity of the sundial, only this time there is something very different about this place. In fact the only thing I recognise is the sundial. I stand and look all around me, where is this place? I appear to be standing on a slopping lawn surrounded by a very low fence on three sides and the wall with the door in it on the other. Is this part of the awakening?

I move cautiously towards the sundial, feeling more certain with every step that I should know this place, but still nothing seems at all familiar. Having reached the sundial still feeling uncertain of my whereabouts and what I can expect, I realise that I am no longer alone here. If Miss Florence has followed me anyway it could be very difficult for all concerned or worse still the awakening will not happen. If this awakening does not happen, will I stop seeing them altogether? I worry. I can't let this happen!

I turn around to try and discover who has joined me, but can see no-one. I realise that either the crying has stopped or, it cannot be heard outside the house. Feeling slightly agitated I turn back towards the door through which I have just entered this place. Still I can see no-one. Why am I here? Am I even in the right place?

'Miss Florence, is that you? Why don't you just come out here and join me?'
The irritation and indignation in my voice is more evident than I had intended it to be. Despite the rustle of leaves all around me and

my certain knowledge that someone else is here with me, still no-one appears.

'If you are following me, please will you either return to the Manor, or come out and make yourself known.'

This time although I try to sound the same, even I can hear the wobble in my voice, giving away my rapidly shrinking confidence. Now there is no movement and no sound, maybe I was imagining it all the time, but wait, no, I am definitely sensing a second presence here. By now I am becoming more nervous than frustrated, but still no-one appears.

'Oh Elsie, where are you? Please help me, I don't know where to go, what to do or even what to think.'

I stand in silence for several minutes. It is only when I place my hands on the sundial, as I had before, that things begin changing.

First the low fences appear to be swallowed up by shrubs, and plants seem to be growing everywhere. The sundial has been here forever, am I seeing ages passing? It is just that when it was first placed here the gardens were different. So, this morning my leaving the Manor was part of the awakening. Does this explain the crying? Still I sense a second presence here with me, maybe now whoever it is will show themselves.

The Diary of Miss Ruby March

After just a very short while, the sundial garden, as I have named it seems to be more familiar to me, or so I think, but then I see a mass of ivy climbing high into the clear blue sky. This has never been here before. I begin to cautiously move away from the sundial towards the tangled mass of tendrils and leaves. As I get closer I can see that beneath the ivy is a tower, or at least what is left of a tower. I stop and gaze at this strange place. I am beginning to feel that I am encroaching on somebody's private space, and yet something is drawing me closer. It is only now I realise that once again I can hear the crying; but this time it is louder than it was at the Manor. It is coming from inside the tower. Could this really be the turret room? But how? The Manor is nowhere to be seen, and the tower behind the ivy is little more than a ruin. None of this makes sense. I move a little closer and can see what appears to be a doorway now, but still I do not enter. Elsie's warning is ringing in my ears.

'Whatever, you hear or think you see, you must not go up there.'

If this truly is the turret room, then to go in would surely be breaking a promise, and yet...

My conflicting thoughts are quickly

interrupted when the crying suddenly stops and from behind the ivy appears a figure. I cannot help but gasp as I recognise her instantly as the flower-clad lady from the bridge, but who is she and why am I seeing her again now? She is not dancing this time. She is simply standing, looking into the distance. Is this the presence I have been sensing all morning?

No, no it isn't, I still believe someone else is here just out of sight, but whom? I continue to watch the maiden, and as before, a second figure appears. There is no water here, but the man from the stream appears, this time out of the ivy. Once again their hands join and bodies entwine, before apparently fading back into the mass of tangled dark green tendrils. Who is this couple? Why am I seeing them? Are they part of the Manor's story? Or my story? A cold shiver runs right through me, this is the first time I have thought about it, but it is something Elsie mentioned last time, about beginning to discover things about my own life. Could this couple be part of that discovery?

The two figures have been gone for a few minutes now, and the crying has not started again, but still I dare not enter the tower. I do move little closer and can now see a window through which dappled light creeps into the tower. The ivy tendrils are not as dense in this window and despite the melancholic appearance of this place the feeling of expectancy and enchantment are greater.

I hear a voice calling to me from behind now.

'Ruby, Ruby are you ready?'

'Oh, oh Miss Charlotte.'

I reply as I spin round expecting to see her, but there is no-one. Desperately I call out.

'Miss Charlotte, where are you?'

'Elsie has sent me to take you to her, but only if you are ready. Are you ready child?'

'Ready for what? I don't understand.'

'I can say no more at present, but if you are ready, you are to enter the tower.'

'But she told me never to enter the turret room, and I heard crying here today?'

'Hush child, this is not the turret room, and only you can decide if you are ready, but know this;

If you can be brave,
And step inside,
Your future seemingly once so grave,
Will begin to change and upwards can glide.
Answers you seek,

The Diary of Miss Ruby March

And knowledge so longed for,
Will seem much less bleak,
As with hope you'll continue through each new
door.

'Oh Miss Charlotte, I don't know what to do, if I step inside I am afraid that everything will change, and I don't know if I want that. I am happy here and for the first time in my life, I am cared for and wanted. But if I don't step inside will I ever know the answers to my many questions.'

'Ruby, I cannot tell you what to do as I have already said, but if you do not feel ready today, then another opportunity will come soon. All your questions will eventually be answered, but should you decide not to come with me now, you need only to turn around and the Manor will appear before you. The choice has to be your own child. Rest assured that whatever you decide, your life will only change when and if you want it too. Your life at the Manor is a safe place while wounds from the past begin to heal. You can stay for as long as you need too, but remember it is only a stepping stone in your life's journey. Now, my time is at an end, you must decide now.'

'Oh Miss Charlotte wait, please wait for me, I am coming.'

The Diary of Miss Ruby March

Before I really know what is happening, I have stepped inside the tower and both Miss Charlotte and Elsie are standing with me.

'I am so glad you have been brave enough to come Ruby, now take my hand our journey together can at last begin.'

Without another word I allow both Elsie and Miss Charlotte to take hold of my hands, and even as they do so, the tower, the ivy and everything surrounding us melts away and we are standing in front of a house. I can feel myself stiffen all over and I can't move.

'Ruby, dearest Ruby do not be afraid, nothing you are seeing or will see can ever hurt you. Any people we may encounter will not know we are here, but for you to fully understand much of what will be made known to you today and in future awakenings, it is important, nay, imperative that you see them. Do you understand child?'

Unable to speak for fear of bursting into tears, I simply nod my head and allow myself to be led towards the house. As we approach I can feel my heart pounding in my chest and my throat feels as though it is constricting with every step. The door is already standing open, and the aroma of freshly baked bread is hanging enticingly on the breeze.

My curiosity and desire for answers finally

gets the better of me, and I can stay silent no longer.

'I thought nobody would know of our presence here Elsie, but it smells like whoever lives here is expecting someone?'

'Indeed they are Ruby, but it is not us, at least…never mind just keep watching and some things at least, I hope will begin to become clear. If this is not the case, myself and Miss Charlotte will explain what we can when we reach our destination.'

'Where are we going?'

Neither Miss Charlotte nor Elsie make any reply, but continue to lead me through the house and out into a garden. It is not a place I know, yet as with the house, somewhere deep in my memory something is stirring. Not exactly a memory, or even a recognition, but something. We stop moving and I watch intently as a very young girl plays contentedly at the feet of a young woman who is sitting and sewing. The young woman is as elegant and delicate as the chair on which she is sitting. It is not until she looks up from her work to smile at the cherub-like child that I recognise her as the flower-clad maiden.

Until now the child has been seated with her back to us, but as her mother, I assume carefully places her fine stitch work on the lace-covered table beside her, the rosy-cheeked child turns to look at her. I can't believe what I am seeing; this delightful child is none other than Elsie herself. I look at Elsie and can see tears glistening on her cheeks as she turns to try and smile at me.

With my voice little more than a whisper I know I have to ask why I am seeing this. Surely this is part of Elsie's story not mine.

'Hush child, keep watching and you will see and understand.'

This I know is supposed to reassure me, but it seems to do the opposite as my fear increases and I begin to doubt whether I really was ready to step inside that tower. As I watch however, another figure appears. Again I recognise him as the man from the water and as of this morning from the ivy, but I still cannot understand why I need to see this. The scene before us is one of pure joy and contentment and one which I longed for as a child. However, this blissful tableau does not last long.

The sky begins to darken and a chill runs through all three of us as we stand and watch. The scene changes, the garden and house are still the same as are Elsie and her mother, except that both are now dressed in black.

Elsie is still very young, although now she is nearer the age I was when I first met her, but her rosy complexion has been replaced by one of pallor and bewilderment reflecting the almost demented grief of her mother. A huge lump comes into my throat as I begin to realise what must have happened. I hear a sniff from beside me, but as my own vision has now blurred with tears I fail to see how I can be of comfort to anyone.

We continue to stand together, as the whole scene changes, the house and garden are replaced by…no, no it can't be. Not that place. I feel my legs begin to tremble and can barely stand. The building I see before me now is the same one I had left only months earlier. I look in desperation to Elsie for comfort, but her grip on my hand just tightens a little while her gaze remains firmly fixed ahead of her.

I have been dreading seeing this place again, but as I continue to watch, I realise it is not me I am watching, but Elsie. She is kneeling beside a narrow hard bed clinging tightly to a limp, lifeless white arm hanging down. As I continue to watch, I realise that the arm belongs to the thin lifeless form of the young woman, hardly recognisable now as Elsie's mother, lying on the bed. Her chest is barely moving as her breathing is shallow, laboured and rasping. After a few seconds it stops altogether and a nurse quickly covers the porcelain-like face, before forcibly and harshly removing a distraught Elsie from the bedside and the room. I can sense Elsie's pain and deep distress beside me, but can do nothing to ease it as I am feeling weaker all the time, and it is taking all my remaining strength to stand here.

Now the scene is changing again, but as it does so I can feel Elsie and Miss Charlotte tugging at my hand to move on. As I do I stumble, nearly landing in a heap on the ground. After I have once again regained my balance, I look up and see a tumbledown cottage surrounded by an, unkempt garden with tangles of weeds and brambles in all directions. The closer I look at this place the more I begin to realise where I am. This is Elsie's childhood home. Why are we back here? Why is it so sad and shabby now? I glance at Elsie, but before I can say anything I notice that one of the now torn lace curtains in one of the bottom two windows is hurriedly replaced. Someone is in there and not wanting to be seen. But I thought people here couldn't see us?

As I continue to watch the curtain

continues to twitch nervously, and I soon become aware that it isn't us the person within is so afraid of, as another figure appears at the gateway opposite us. It is a figure that has always filled me with nothing but horror. My uncle, I gasp as he draws nearer. I cannot help but giggle nervously as a playful gust of wind catches the rim of his hat lifting it completely off his prematurely balding head and placing it carefully a thorny tangle of weeds and brambles. His facial expression is one of annoyance and irritation, but the sight of him trying to retrieve it from its resting place means my giggle turns into audible laughter, and even Elsie and Miss Charlotte are trying to conceal their obvious amusement.

It is only once he has regained his usual stern, upright demeanour that the peculiarity of this scene really starts to become obvious to me. Why is my uncle, or at least the man I have always known as my uncle here? What possible connection can he have to Elsie's childhood home? Now reality is beginning to take over once more as nothing but unanswered questions crowd into my already dizzy head. Then the most uncomfortable question of all, who is hiding in this house? Why are they so afraid of this man?

The Diary of Miss Ruby March

Fear is once more the overwhelming feeling inside of me as well, and the relief of a few moments ago is but a rapidly fading memory. He approaches the door and knocks abruptly and with great purpose. I can sense that Elsie and Miss Charlotte are feeling uneasy. The atmosphere becomes almost suffocating.

My uncle's irritation at the lack of response to his knocking is evident to all of us. Then he speaks, and even as the words leave his mouth my blood turns cold, not only at the sound of his heartless voice, but also at the words I hear.

'You may be able to hide here for now, but I will be coming back, and you know very well that when I return you will have no choice. You will come with me, and you will do it willingly, if not for yourself then for the sake of the child you will soon bear.'

The three of us stand in silence and watch as this terrifying man turns with a flourish and strides purposefully away. Elsie turns to face me and asks the hardest question I have ever faced.

'Dearest Ruby, you have already been so brave this morning, before we continue you need to know that if you choose to continue further today, you can never and will never be the same. Everything you have ever known or believed to be true will be challenged enormously. I cannot tell you what to do but whatever you decide, remember this;

> *The time and friendship we have shared,*
> *Both here and in the past,*
> *Will never have to alter,*
> *And will for ever last.*

The future holds exciting but very different times for all of us. If today you do not feel able to continue I will understand. However if you do decide you are brave enough to keep going, all I ask is that you will not let the truths you discover come between us. None of what lies ahead can be made known to you until you are ready, and only you can decide whether you are.'

I stand looking into the face of my dearest friend; the longer I look the more I am convinced that her eyes show a deep yearning to be able to share something greater with me.

'Oh Elsie, I don't know what to do. I am so confused, as all I have seen so far this morning appears to be part of your story and separate from my own. That is until my uncle appeared. Why would he be here at your childhood home, and who is living here now? I don't understand.'

'Oh Ruby, I do so wish that I could simply give you the answers you seek, but I fear that if I were to do this, the future would not be one that either of us want. The answers you seek are closer than you realise, but you have to see everything to fully understand. If we are to continue today, we must do it quickly as there is much to see and time is short. If you decide instead that you want to wait, your journey back begins and ends here. What is your decision Ruby?'

I glance towards Miss Charlotte and back towards Elsie not knowing what to do. I want so much to continue and know the truths and answers that are ahead, but I am fearful and perturbed by Elsie's words about the future being unwanted. I don't want to lose the only true friend I have known throughout my life.

As we stand there the wind increases and the curtain twitches more and more.

'Ruby, you must decide now, the awakening is coming to an end unless we move on now.'

The urgency in Elsie's voice is palpable and unlike at the tower earlier, I step forward much more willingly this time. As I do so the fear I feel is so intense I have to close my eyes tightly to control it, as I hear a door shudder and creak open from its warped frame and on its rusty hinges. With my eyes still closed I sense the light dim significantly as we enter, what I assume to be, the tumbledown cottage.

'Are you alright Ruby? Open your eyes child; there is nothing here for you to fear. You have made a brave decision Ruby, the journey we have embarked on today will be rocky at times and will not conclude quickly, but for you to fully understand the truth, it is a road which must be travelled.'

With Elsie's reassurance and the certain knowledge that I am not alone, I slowly open my eyes. The room I find myself in is small dimly lit, and sparsely furnished with everything looking tired and unloved. An atmosphere of melancholy and heartache hang heavily here. It isn't until my eyes become properly adjusted to the dim, flickering light of a tiny single candle that I even see the small waif-like figure sitting huddled in a threadbare blanket on a simple wooden stool by the window. When I do, it does not take me more than a few seconds to recognise her as Elsie. Unable to stop myself, I gasp and stare helplessly at my friend. The obvious fear and distress in the face of this other Elsie is reflected deeply in that of the

Elsie standing beside me.

'Oh Elsie, whatever happened here? Why are you back here so alone and frightened? When did you leave that other place?'

'Dearest Ruby, I fled from there as soon as I could. You understand why child as you have been there yourself, but the world is not a safe place for a child of barely fifteen years as I was soon to discover, and I knew my only option was to return here until…'

'Until what? Elsie, please don't stop.'

'That is for another time child but I knew when I did, I would be tracked down and given the choice you witnessed only a few moments ago.'

'But that man is my Uncle, why would he be after you? How would he even know you?'

As we continue to stand here, I hear Elsie on the stool talking to herself. The harder I listen the more I realise that what she is saying is almost poetic and tells of the sorrow she bears.

I stare beyond but do not see,
What lies outside is not for me,
The cobweb curtains mar the view,
I no longer see the sky so blue.

The Diary of Miss Ruby March

I sit in fear inside this house,
But take some comfort as I watch a mouse,
Scamper behind the tattered nets,
Only a glimmer of mottled light in gets.

My hope alone is as I sit here,
Shedding many a silent tear,
That all the cobwebs, dirt and grime,
Will block others from viewing my silent crime.

A knock at the door, oh no, not him,
My hope of remaining here grows dim,
The cobweb shrouds and remnants of net,
Behind windows of grime, I am vulnerable yet.

Beside me Elsie says nothing more, but smiles weakly and, letting go of my hand, places an arm around my shoulders and pulls me closer to her.

The three of us continue to stand in this place so full of memories and sadness as the scene changes again. We are no longer inside the tumble down cottage, but halfway down the long driveway leading to my Uncle's property. Coming towards us is a thin, pale figure barely recognisable as Elsie, but Elsie it is. As we continue to watch she stops, turns and walks back towards the house before stopping again and running past us in the opposite direction, as fast as she can. It I only now I see the tiny form of a baby held tightly to her. We turn quickly to see the tumbledown cottage once more as it melts away to reveal the hateful place I had left only months earlier. The place that shaped both Elsie's life, and my own. However, this time all I see is the great door close behind Elsie as she enters, but I knew she was not alone. Who was with her I knew not, but I know I caught the most fleeting glimpse of another figure ahead of her, much smaller than she was. Elsie had entered with her head bowed, her shoulders slumped and her feet dragging with every step.

'Oh Elsie, I do not understand, what has any of this to do with me? I know and understand now that we have both suffered in silence for many years at the hands of the same cruel people, and that for a short time we were thrown together at my Uncle's house, but the rest is as mysterious as it ever has been. You looked so sad, as that door closed behind you, and I know how that feels too, I just want to understand.'

'Come child, dry your eyes, I think that is enough for today. But, I will say this; I knew that once the door of that hateful place slammed shut behind me there was to be no turning back. But, I also knew I had no other choice. You are right in your observations Ruby, just the thought of what I was doing made me feel sick, as I rang the bell and heard its distant chime summoning the person who would grant us admittance. This very date would always herald a point in my life I would never forget…

Ruby, whatever is it child?'

The feeling of bewilderment I know at this minute must show on my face, or why would Elsie ask such a question?

'Just now you talked about 'us', but I thought you were alone here, what did you mean? Who was with you?'

There is a silence as all the colour drains from Elsie's face as she looks at me with a look of wanting to say something, but not being able too.

'Oh Ruby, I did indeed say us and I should not have done. There was indeed someone else with me, someone very precious indeed, but I cannot say more yet. Believe me dearest Ruby, I would like nothing more than to tell you everything now, but that is not a good idea. Please be patient for a short while longer.'

Her pleading is from the heart and I can

see real fear in her eyes as she begs this of me. So, reluctantly I agree.

'Now Ruby, it is time for you to return to the Manor, but I am concerned that you are still too distressed and confused. Will you be alright child?'

'I…I think so, but I still don't know why I am seeing all this and I do feel shaky, but whenever I return, I always feel better after a while.'

I say this as much to convince myself as Elsie, and she seems to sense this, as what happens next has never happened before.

'Miss Charlotte will accompany you as far as the main door child, from now on I am never far away. If you need me I will be just around the next corner. Dearest Ruby, until we meet again and are able to continue this journey together.'

My eyes barely blink, but immediately the Manor is before us and only two figures are approaching, myself and Miss Charlotte.

'You must go on alone now Ruby, but remember all that you have seen and heard today. You will find comfort in it soon child.'

With that Miss Charlotte is gone and I am once more alone. I suddenly remember that I had left through the rear door this morning to avoid Miss Florence coming with me. Unsure what to do now, I make my way carefully round to the back of the Manor and enter through the door from which I had made my exit earlier. It is only now, as I make my way to the front staircase, that I realise I have returned at the same moment at which I had left. I don't think I will ever understand the difference in time between here and during the awakenings, but at least it means I can go out now with Miss Florence in the knowledge that nothing untoward will occur.

The Diary of Miss Ruby March

30 May 1877

Ever since that day, when my whole life began to change, the sounds and noises of the Manor seem to be increasing and intensifying by the day. But tonight as I climb the stairs to my room, there is a new feeling about the place, one which makes me feel uneasy as I reach the door of my room. Night times here have never really frightened me before; I have always found them to be peaceful and almost comforting. But not tonight, I cannot escape the feeling that sleep is not going to come easy to me. In fact something inside me is leading me to believe that the next awakening will happen tonight. I have never left the Manor at night and do not feel inclined to do so now, but as I climb into bed, this feeling only increases.

Pulling the covers tightly around me I find myself clinging to them for comfort so hard that my fingers begin to go numb. I have not yet dared to extinguish my candle, although the shadows it is casting around the room, is not serving to comfort me at all. I begin to think that no light may be more comforting, so I blow out the flickering flame expecting the shadows to disappear, but they do not. My room begins to grow lighter, not darker, and I am sure I can hear singing. Not the type of singing that is reassuring, but the type that I used to sing when I was alone and frightened as a child to try and cheer myself up. It never worked then, it is certainly not working now. With my mouth as dry as paper, and my throat feeling so tight it is as though I am choking, I decide that my only choice is to wrap myself in my dressing gown and a blanket, and leave my room once more to find the source of the singing. The minute I step out into the corridor everything is silent and at peace once more. This makes no sense, why should I hear singing in my room and there be silence outside it? I stand and wait for several minutes in case I should hear it again. But, after a while I can feel myself calming a little and my eyes are becoming heavy with sleep.

I return to my room and open the door, trembling as I do so in case it is as I had left it a short while ago. But, to my relief everything appears to be draped in a comforting cloak of darkness with only the usual creaks and whimpers that accompany a house such as this. Climbing back into bed I finally begin to drift off to sleep.

With a terrifying start, I am once more wide awake; at first I think it must be morning. I stretch and make my way to the window to peer through the curtains, I realise it is still night and only a few moments have passed. I glance at the large clock above the fire place; in fact no time has passed at all. It is telling the same time as when I first arrived in my room to go to bed. This has to be an awakening, nothing else makes sense. But why at night? This has never happened before and I wish it wasn't happening now. Usually I look forward to these awakenings. This feels different, more sinister, dangerous even. In spite of the time of year being summer, as I leave my bed for the second time tonight, I feel chilled to the bone. Instead of going out into the corridor, I find myself being drawn towards the tall bookcase at the far side of my room. There seems to be light glowing all around it. Is this a secret door, or is it…? Before I can answer these questions for myself the whole room shakes violently as the great bookcase turns to the side granting access to what lies beyond.

My fear is intense but I cannot stop myself from being drawn in, into this huge space which opened as if by magic.

'Elsie, Miss Charlotte, help me please? Where are you? I…'
My words dry up as I see before me a place I

know well, of cruelty, hatred and loathing.

'No, NO! Not here, why do I have to go back here? I cannot face this again.'

Falling to my knees I begin to sob until I am so exhausted, I can sob no more. With my eyes red and sore I lift my head and look up hoping it was just a bad dream, but no, I am still there, only now I am not alone.

'Ruby, Ruby, come child, you have nothing here now, no-one can hurt you anymore.'

I know the sweet, gentle voice at once.

'Elsie, is that you?'

My own voice is little more than a croaky whisper. As my vision begins to clear a little I can see her standing in front of me.

'Come child, tonight your fears will at last begin to leave you, but for this to happen you have to see something first.'

'Is Miss Charlotte not coming with us this time, Elsie?'

'Not this time child, this time it is right for it to be just the two of us.'

Without another word Elsie takes my hands in her own and helps me to my feet, before guiding me to the place before us, the place of my worst nightmares and the one place I never wanted to return too. As we enter through the imposing, unforgiving front door into the dimly lit hallway, the very smell of the place brings back painful memories for me. But this time something feels different. I know I am not alone because Elsie is with me, but it is more than that, I just don't know yet what it is.

We make our way down the long corridor towards a room I know only too well, but as we reach the door, I freeze and can go no further.

'Oh Elsie, I can't go in there, I can't. What happens if we are caught? The punishment here is severe; you and I both know that.'

'It is alright child we are quite safe, as with the last awakening, no-one here can see or hear us. They will never know we have even been here, I promise.'

In spite of Elsie's reassurances, as she turns the handle and the door begins to open, I can feel myself tighten all over. It is only as we enter the room and the door closes behind us, that I realise I have also been holding my breath. I release it and sigh deeply, trying to keep calm.

The room is empty apart from the large desk and enormous leather-clad chair behind it, where the Matron always sits, only now there is no sign of her. This is not a disappointment to me, as just the sight of her tall, severe, almost starched appearance has always been enough to send shivers right through me. While I stand in the middle of this vast cavern of a room trying to decide where to go, Elsie is already busy searching every drawer and box she can find.

'What are you looking for Elsie? Can I help?'

But she makes no response. Maybe she didn't hear me, I know I spoke in little more than a whisper, however, with the room so still and silent I thought it would be impossible not to hear.

'Elsie are you alright? Have you lost something? What can I do?'

Again she makes no reply, but after a few more seconds she stops and, clutching something close to her chest, she returns to my side.

'I'm sorry Ruby; I knew that I had to search for this myself. I could not tell you what to look for as I had no idea myself what it looked like. But now I have it, come on.'

'Can we leave-?'

Before I can even finish the question I am being hurriedly up the stairs to the attic rooms. We are obviously not leaving, but why are we going up here? No-one ever went up here, even as a punishment. There was only one time I saw someone coming down from the attic, and that was …., the memory was all too vivid in my head. I remembered the tiny child almost tumbling down the stairs in front of Matron, as they were hurriedly taken to a room where only minutes later they left with a man and a woman not to be seen again. But I never knew why they had been up here, or even who the child was. The only other thing I remember about that day is the sound of distant crying. Who had been crying? I never discovered, but many of us shed tears frequently in this place, so crying was often heard in many directions.

We have reached the very top of the building now and the only light came from under a small door at the far end of a very dark, narrow corridor. Elsie stops, and I am glad of the rest, but there is something about Elsie now which I have only seen once before, when my Uncle appeared at her childhood home.

'Elsie, are you alright? Why have you brought me here? Can't we go back now?'

'Oh Ruby, I too am afraid. Afraid, that if I take you through that door with me all that we have shared and the friendship we have known will be lost forever. I am also afraid that you may still not understand all that you are seeing and why, but if we turn back now...'

'What? What will happen if we turn back now, and why would our friendship be lost? Oh Elsie, you are scaring me.'

For several minutes the two of us stand silent and motionless not even looking at each other, but at the door to the room we are facing. Then, still without a word, Elsie takes my hand and slowly we move closer to the door. Stopping again only a few feet away, I ask again.

'Elsie, what will happen if we turn back without seeing what is behind the door?''

'Dearest Ruby, if you do not see this tonight, it will only delay what has to be.'

'But I don't want things to change between us, why can't we just keep them the way they are?'

'Dear child, if we kept everything as it is now, you would never find all the answers you are seeking. We have to continue this journey, whether that is now or at another time. It is vital that you discover the truth about who you really are and what has brought you here. There are reasons behind all the things you have been through Ruby, and most important of all is the truth that lies behind this door. Whatever happens and whatever you decide, you must know that I will always be here for you and will never stop caring about you.

Now, are we going to continue, or are you going to return to the Manor without knowing anymore than you did when this awakening started? The choice is yours, but if you go back today you will have to return here again next time. Would you not rather put this part behind you?'

Elsie is right; I do of course want to put this place and all my memories of it behind me. But there is a fear in her which is making me not want to do it.

I stand with my gaze fixed on the door unable to move forwards or backwards, until eventually Elsie takes my hands and turns to face me.

'Ruby, our time here tonight grows short, what are you going to do?'

Pleadingly I beg Elsie not to abandon me.

'Will you come with me? Please say that you will stay and not leave my side?'

'I will come Ruby, I have too, but whether I stay will be up to you. This is where your story truly begins and the answers you seek can finally begin to reveal themselves. Will you come with me now? Your future awaits.'

With my heart pounding and my legs not wanting to move, I allow myself to be guided slowly the remaining short distance towards the door. As Elsie turns the handle, I close my eyes to what lies beyond, but as I enter the room, I can feel the atmosphere change. For the first time tonight there is a sense of expectation and almost joy in the place, although the heaviness of misery and fear is not far away. I hear the door close behind me, and realise now that Elsie has let go of my hands.

'Elsie, Elsie where are you? You said you would be with me, please come back.'
In desperation and fear I open my eyes and frantically search the gloomy room for my friend.

'It's alright Ruby I'm here, you are quite safe.'
I turn to find her standing against the door.

'Oh please Elsie stand with me, I don't think I can face this alone.'

'You must see all that this room contains, and you must see it without me being too close. I cannot influence this in any way. But, I do promise that when you have seen all that is contained here, I will be

113

waiting and, if you want to we can leave together.'

'But…'

'I can say no more now, just take a look and please try to understand.'

Realising that I have very little choice, I turn away from the door and slowly begin to move across the room towards a small bed. Beside this bed a single candle flickers and flutters as a draught from the tiny attic window tries unsuccessfully to extinguish the flame. As I get nearer I can see a very young child sleeping fitfully on the bed. No, it can't be, but yes it is, there is Elsie herself sitting beside this bed on a tiny wooden stool, humming gently as though trying to soothe the restless, but sleepy infant.

'I …I don't understand Elsie, what am I seeing here?'

'Keep watching Ruby, this is just the beginning.'

As I continue to watch, the scene begins to change and I realise for the first time, that the child I had seen all those years ago being dragged down the stairs was not something I had seen, but something I had experienced. With a gasp and a stifled sob, I realise that the child is me, and it was a memory which, until now, I had blocked out and distanced myself from; hence believing I had seen it instead.

I glance back towards the bed. It is now empty; Elsie is still beside the bed alone now.

'But I thought you didn't know me until we met at my Uncles when I was four or five? I am glad you cared for me here too, I wouldn't have wanted anyone else, I always feel comfortable with you.'

As I say this however, I notice that the Elsie on the stool is sobbing as she packs her few possessions into a tiny case and leaves the scene. Glancing back towards the door, I see that Elsie who had come with me is also crying bitterly.

Oh, Elsie, please don't, what is it? Why are you crying? Have I done something wrong?'

'No Ruby, you have done nothing child, it is just that... well perhaps that is for another time. Are you ready?'

'Are we going now? Is this awakening also at an end?'

'We are leaving this place Ruby, at least for now, but the awakening will only end when you want it too.'

I really do not understand what this means, however, I am glad to escape from this place at last. So happy to be at Elsie's side once more, I leave the attic room behind me, and as we leave the whole scene changes and we find ourselves back in the garden of Elsie's cottage.

'I had begun to think I would never see this place again, please may I stay with you for a while?'

'Ruby, you have another choice to make now, you must know by now that you are always welcome here, but if you want to fully understand all that you have seen today we could go on to the next place. You must decide.'

Now the tears which I had been fighting back finally begin to escape, and I know I have seen enough for today.

'I think I would like to rest a while please Elsie, I am so tired.'

We enter the friendly little cottage and this time instead of taking my usual seat at the table, Elsie tells me to make my way to the large armchair beside the other window.

'Dearest Ruby, you rest here and I will fetch some tea.'

As I sink back into the luxurious soft cushions, I know I will not be able to keep my eyes open for long. This awakening is after all taking place in the middle of the night. Only now do I think about standing in the garden a few moments ago. If it is the middle of the night, why were we standing in daylight? I know that time during awakenings is different from that at the Manor, but the time of day has always appeared to be the same. Although confused by this, I am now so tired, and my eyes so heavy, that sleep is inevitable.

I wake eventually and to begin with am completely disorientated. Slowly I begin to recognise the pretty lace curtains and comforting aroma of lavender from outside the front of Elsie's cottage. A freshly brewed pot of tea stands on the table with the usual jug of milk and two cups, but there is no sign of Elsie. It is only now that I have been at least partially awake for several minutes, that the aroma of lavender begins to make any sense. I am now aware that the door which had been closed behind us when we entered the cottage is standing wide open.

Why would Elsie just disappear like this? Rising stiffly from the armchair, I stretch and shake myself in an attempt to fully wake up. This is largely unsuccessful, but at least now I can make my way outside. I reach the door of the cottage and stare out into the garden, but can see no-one. This is not only because there is no-one out there to see, but night appears to have caught up and darkness shrouds the garden. With a shiver and a growing sense of foreboding, I return inside the cottage and make my way to the table. It is only now that I see a note propped up against the teapot and the plain white envelope beneath it. Why could I not see that the light in here had changed? The flickering candles and dancing shadows are obvious to me now.

Picking up the note, I move closer to one of the candles and can just about make out my name. I unfold the paper and with some difficulty manage to read the message it contains.

The words I read make me feel numb. After a few moments, in spite of my ever growing thirst, I leave the tea in the pot and, picking up the white envelope from the table, I leave the cottage. Something tells me that this white envelope is the same thing that Elsie herself looked so frantically for earlier, and on finding it held it close to her from that point on. Close, that is, until now. Why leave it for me? As the door closes and I take my first step into the inky blackness, the Manor appears in front of me. With a growing sense of confusion and fear, I return once more to my room. Climbing back into bed, the room is still dark and quiet, unlike when I had left it, but the clock is still indicating the same time. Time has been frozen. How is this even possible? Why would Elsie leave such a strange, almost cryptic message? Who am I? This last question is the most disturbing and unsettling of all, but once again my eyes are heavy with sleep and in spite of myself, I am soon drifting off, albeit fitfully, once more.

This time when I wake up a deafening chorus of birdsong can be clearly heard, and the sun is already rising. Glancing at the clock, I am relieved to see that the time has changed, but realise instantly that this morning I will not be walking anywhere before breakfast, surprisingly this feels alright with me. I climb out of bed and begin to ready myself for the day ahead; it is then that I catch sight of the strange note and white envelope from last night. With a shudder I stop and read Elsie's message once more. It still makes no sense, but somehow my fear is less intense in daylight. Trying to push any thoughts about last night to the back of my mind, I slip the note and the envelope into the pocket of my pinafore before making my way downstairs to breakfast.

The Diary of Miss Ruby March

20 June 1877

The next few days pass uneventfully and are surprisingly enjoyable. Spring is now rapidly giving way to summer, and with the ever-lengthening days, Miss Florence is continually at my side. She is always up and ready before me in the mornings.

That is until this morning. Today I am wide awake just as the grey light of dawn is beginning to show in the sky. I had all but forgotten about the note and envelope in the pocket of my pinafore, but this morning, as I lay here thinking about how to escape outside without Miss Florence, I remember them. Silently as I can I make my way across the room and feel in the pocket. A cold shiver runs right through me, they are no longer there. Panic grips me. By the dim early morning light, I begin searching everywhere. I know I have to find them before I can go any further. I move things frantically from one place to another and back again several times, but no sign can I find of either the note or the envelope.

Eventually, feeling thoroughly exhausted, devoid of hope and with tears of desperation blurring my vision, I return to my pinafore. Grabbing it viciously, and toss it forcefully onto the floor. As I try to calm down, I notice, poking out from under the corner of my pretty desk is a corner of paper. Easing it out gently using the tip of my finger I see the familiar writing.

How did it get here? With the note found, I begin to regain my hope of finding the envelope. Picking up my pinafore from its resting place on the floor, I see the envelope slightly further under the desk. My hand will not quite fit underneath, so I begin looking around for something I can use to retrieve it with. To begin with I can find nothing, but then I remember the night of the awakening.

I make my way across the room to the bookcase, and, reaching in beside it, find the long peacock feather I recalled seeing there that night. My first few attempts at swishing out the envelope from its hiding place achieve nothing more than creating a huge dust cloud which covers me and the desk, however eventually I hear the feather catch the paper, and the envelope as well as another lot of dust and cobwebs comes skidding out across the floor.

By now the first light of dawn has given way to early sunshine, and I hurriedly ready myself to attempt to make my escape. Descending the stairs as silently as possible, I pause, hardly daring to breathe, as I reach Miss Florence's room. It appears to be safe. I quicken my pace and, not daring to risk the front door, make my way quickly to the back of the house and out into the garden.

This time as I begin to read the delicately written message, I feel different about it. I know instantly that today I will see another awakening. This time the words begin to appear less jumbled, although I still don't understand what it all means.

Darling Ruby,

Today your future has begun,
But I must depart before the sun,
You know that you are welcome here,
And that you never need to fear,
But when you leave please take this with you,
And keep it close the words are true,
The envelope has what you need to know,
Allow its truth to help you grow,
But only open it when you are strong,
I had no choice, I did not belong,
Keep it safe and close to your heart,
When you know, your life can start.
You control the time and place,
When you know we may both need space,
But until that time I'll be waiting near,

The Diary of Miss Ruby March

Never wanting you to fear,
It may not be before we meet again,
That you read the cause of so much pain,
But rest assured you'll always be,
The one who means the most to me.

By the time I reach the end of the second read through, I am crying, although I am not certain why. Seeing the sun now well above the horizon I realise that I am not yet out of sight of the Manor, and therefore still at risk of being joined by an irate Miss Florence, demanding to know why I had left without her. The scent from the roses and many other flowers is quite intoxicating this morning, as I make my way across the formal courtyard towards the far side, only this time I don't get more than halfway across before I hear the gate. The same gate which had allowed my escape from Master Edward the first time I found myself here. Glancing round quickly, I almost expect to see Miss Florence standing there, instead I see no-one, but know from the now open gate that this is the way I have to proceed. So, changing direction I make my way to the gate and pass through it, expecting to find the wilderness that I had entered before, but although the path is the same, my surroundings could not be more different with neatly trimmed hedges and flowering shrubs. This time I find myself standing in a place I feel I should recognise but don't. However, I find myself being drawn to a huge tree in the centre.

The whole atmosphere in this place seems almost solemn, not to say sombre, compared to the pretty formal courtyard I have just left. I make my way to the tree, looking around me all the time hoping to see or hear something, but nothing, there is silence and nobody. On reaching the tree I am full of expectation which fades as nothing appears to change or happen. I stand for several minutes under the vast canopy fearing I have made a mistake and taken the wrong path when, on a branch just above my head, a bird begins to sing before fluttering down and landing on, what until now has been a hidden door.

This door is narrow but intricately carved with an ivy pattern making the tiny wooden handle almost impossible to see. Before I even place my hand upon it, the door slowly opens. Not to reveal a dark hollow trunk as I expect, but instead a long, beautifully manicured drive with a large stone lion at either side of it. What lies at the end I cannot see, but stepping through I already know I am where I need to be. Unlike previous awakenings where I could still see the place I have come from, this time the door closes behind me and together with the enormous tree is completely concealed from my vision.

Seeing only the long drive stretching endlessly ahead of me I begin to make my way along it. Unlike the place with the huge tree from whence I have just come, this place I am certain is completely unknown to me. Every step I take seems insignificant compared to the distance I still have to travel, but still I continue. The silence and sombre nature of the place is stirring in me a level of anxiety greater than that which I had felt in the place with the tree, but still something compels me to continue along this seemingly never ending drive.

At last I catch my first glimpse of a house. I stop unable to breathe or move. No, no it can't be, not here, not now. I had been so sure I did not know this place as I started along the drive, why can't I remember? Gripped by fear, everything in me is telling me to turn and run, run back the way I have just come, and faster than I have ever run before, but still I cannot move. As I stand here frozen and barely breathing, I begin to sense that I am no longer alone.

'Elsie, Elsie is that you? Please tell me

you have come to take me away from this place?'

There is no answer, and my fear only increases. I am definitely not alone any longer, but if Elsie is here why is she not answering me? I continue to wait and watch, the stark, black, imposing image of my Uncles house looming threateningly ahead like some stifling thick black cloak that is too heavy and almost suffocates me under its weight.

I can hear soft footsteps coming from behind me, but still nobody speaks and I am too terrified to turn and look. The footsteps stop and now I am aware that there is not only one other person beside me, but I now have two companions standing one on either side of me.

'Elsie, Miss Charlotte, please say you are here with me?'
My voice is little more than a whisper, but I dare not repeat myself, so I wait in the uncomfortable silence for someone to respond, but nothing.

If my companions are not Elsie and Miss Charlotte, who are they? Are they even to be trusted? What is this awakening telling me? As my mind begins whirling, searching for something, anything that makes sense, my fear overwhelms me. I feel my legs buckle under me and I fall to the ground. However, my landing is soft and warm, not at all what I am expecting as I am standing on a sharp gravel drive. It is only now I realise my eyes have closed. I want to open them, but am afraid of what I might see when I do. Strangely, I feel safer and more secure than I have since I left the manor this morning, and fear that if I open my eyes this feeling may be ruthlessly shattered, but I also know I cannot remain here for long. Something deep inside is already urging me to continue, so in spite of myself I force my eyes to open.

Nothing could have prepared me for the sight that fills them. It is no little wonder that my landing has been soft and warm, for I find myself nestled across the paws of two huge lions, both purring gently and deeply whilst gazing at me with what can only be described as concern and pity. Unable to stop myself I clamber quickly to my feet and step away from the two great cats with fear, yet I do not really feel threatened by them. Looking all about me and seeing nobody else, I slowly begin to realise that these magnificent creatures must have been my two companions. I stand a small distance away from them, and carefully positioned to ensure I am out of sight of the house, I begin to try to make sense of any of this awakening, but I cannot. Oh how I wish Elsie or Miss Charlotte were here, I need someone to talk to about all this.

As I stand, pondering my next move with my eyes staring upwards at a cloudless blue sky, I should feel warm and at peace on this summer day, but I do not. There is a harsh almost macabre feeling pressing in on me now, and my fear is rapidly overwhelming again. This time however, I do not collapse as before but find myself being gently nuzzled and urged on by my two companions.

Still uncertain whether they are to be trusted or not even though they caught me when I fell, I cannot work out whether they are accompanying me as friends or leading me towards danger and into a trap. I try to fight the gentle persuasion but it is no use, I am moving towards that house. A place of torment and heartache, sorrow and sadness, but also the place where I first remember meeting Elsie. A sudden rush of hope floods through me like a force of energy I have never felt before. Will I finally get to see her here, in this awakening? Or is this something I must face and endure alone? Where did the lions come from? I stop, hardly believing the crazy thoughts racing round my head.

The Diary of Miss Ruby March

'Don't be ridiculous Ruby; stone lions don't suddenly come to life.'
I had not meant to say this out loud, and even I find it hard not to giggle nervously at this most bizarre notion.

Both lions are now urging me forward and no matter how hard I try, I am powerless to stop them. The house is now towering above me and the imposing front door is already standing open. Am I expected here? I turn to look at the lions but they are not there, so why am I still moving forward?

'Ruby, remember what I told you the first time we were reunited during your first awakening and do not be fearful. There is nothing here that can hurt you now, but there are answers if you are prepared to seek them.'

'Elsie, is that you? Where are you? Why can't I see you?'

'All in good time Ruby, but first you must enter the house and make your way to the room in which you stayed.'

'Oh Elsie, I can't do this alone, why can't you come with me?'

'But child, I am with you, it is only that as yet I am not visible to you here, the reason for that will become clear, but only when you reach that room. You must trust me Ruby.'

'I do trust you Elsie, I just wish I could

see you, have you beside me when I go in here.'

I wait several minutes, but Elsie's voice responds no more. I know what I have to do, and I really do trust Elsie, but still my fear is almost overtaking me with every step. By the time I reach the shadow of the doorway itself, I can barely breathe and I feel my heart pounding in my ears.

I freeze in the doorway at the sound of my Aunts voice in the room just inside on my right. That voice has always sent a feeling like shards of ice chasing through my veins, but who is she shouting at? I thought I was the only one who incurred such wrath from her, but the other voice is indistinct and muffled. I know it, or at least I think I do, but cannot put a name to it, at least not yet. Feeling slightly relieved that my Aunt is occupied, I make my way as quickly and as silently as I can up to the tiny attic room where I spent most of my time at this place. The only time I saw the outside was on a Sunday, and then only because my Aunt and Uncle felt obliged to take me with them when they went to church. I was forced to sit between them, and if I so much as breathed at the wrong time it resulted in a beating on our return to the house. I soon learnt that my best course of action was to sit with my head bowed and my hands in my lap for the whole time I was there. Although this never seemed to completely meet with their approval, at least it spared me a beating.

I arrive at the attic and open the door. On entering this dark, dingy, austere place, I almost find some comfort as I close the door behind me. At least while I was up here, I was fairly safe and could escape into my increasingly vivid imagination. Apart from my visits from Elsie, my imagination was my only joy in this place. For four whole years this had been my routine, but now, being back here I remember everything so vividly that it is almost like being that tiny child all over again.

Slowly I begin moving across the room to the tiny cot-like bed that I remember so clearly, when the door opens behind me. Not daring to turn round for fear of who might see, I stop and wait. As I continue to listen, I realise that the footsteps approaching me are too light to be those of an adult, so I turn to see who has joined me. Facing me is the tear-stained face of a tiny waif-like child as alone and friendless as I had been before Elsie arrived.

'Hello little one, please don't be afraid,

I will not hurt you. I know only too well what you are going through.'

My voice is little more than a whisper for fear of being heard, but with the echo up here she could not have failed to her me, and yet there is no recognition of my presence at all. She just continues to come towards me and then past me before climbing, trembling into the bed and hiding herself beneath the threadbare blanket just as I used to do. As I continue to watch her trembling form, a sickening reality begins to dawn on me. The reason she could not see or hear me is because I am watching myself just as Elsie had done.

Why am I seeing this? I know only too well what I went through here; I don't need to see it all again. However, as I continue to stand here the whole scene begins to change and I now find myself, not in the attic room, but in a much grander more lavish room that I have never seen before. Looking all around me I see that I am surrounded by toys of the highest quality, and slowly become aware of a child crying bitterly. I have never known or seen such luxury and fail to understand why any child with such a life would be crying like that. Seeing a crib in the farthest corner, I make my way, slowly, over to the tiny infant. I do not fully know this child, yet something about them is vaguely familiar. I cannot even work out whether they are a boy or a girl. After several more minutes the door to this room opens and a severe, black-clad lady enters, snatches up the screaming child and briskly bustles her way back out of the room. I do not recognise her, but I am certain that she is not the child's mother.

As I stand there my surroundings change again and the toys are gone, replaced by formal furniture but on a smaller than normal scale. Sitting at a desk is a young boy with his back to me. Feeling sure I cannot be seen or heard, I move closer and stand at his side. That face, it can't be, but it is. This young boy is my Uncle, and now I know that the infant from before was also him. As I watch I can see how unhappy and alone he appears to be, and for the first time in my life, I begin to pity him. This feels so strange, but now my tormentor appears to have been the tormented. Again the door opens and this time it is my Aunt who appears, only she is young and beautiful, although her expression is hard and cold. Behind her there is another child, tiny and fragile-looking but instantly recognisable. Unable to stop myself, I gasp, as I see Elsie. But this makes no sense. Then I remember seeing a scene so harrowing I had wanted to look away, that of the death of Elsie's mother. So, does this explain the connection between Elsie and my Aunt and Uncle? But now I can see that my Aunt appears to be so much older than my Uncle, why he is barely more than a child and yet…

My mind is suddenly yanked back to my vision of me being taken from one place of torment by two complete strangers, to another. As a child, it had never occurred to me that anything was strange about these two people who I always thought to be a couple, but seeing this now, I have so many questions.

Hearing the door open behind me, I find myself being sharply brought back to reality, but this time there is no need for me to fear.

'Ruby, are you ready? I think perhaps you have seen enough for today child, come, take my hand and let me take you to a place where you can always feel safe.'

'Elsie, you are here at last.'

'Hush now, you must be exhausted, and in need of a rest.'

Within seconds I find myself once more at Elsie's cottage and able to rest without fear. However, I do not rest for long before Elsie is asking me about what I have discovered today, and whether I understand all that I have seen.

'Oh Elsie, I don't really know what I have discovered; only what I have seen and I certainly do not understand all of that.'

Elsie smiles at me with one of her all knowing smiles, taking a seat opposite me she continues.

'Well then Ruby, why don't you tell me what you have seen, or think you may have seen and together we will try and work out at least part of what it means?'

I am slightly confused by this, what can she mean by think I saw and how can I be of any help in unravelling a mystery that has already left me so utterly confused. Nevertheless, I begin to tell her all that has happened during this awakening so far, including the stone lions that apparently come to life.

'Oh Elsie, what does all this mean?'

'What do you think it means Ruby? Let us begin with the long walk along the drive, what do you think you discovered while doing this?

I look at Elsie and cannot even begin to answer, her question has completely stunned me, what does she mean? My face must display my disbelief and shock as it is Elsie who speaks again.

'Well, why do you think you did not

arrive at the house instantly when you came through the doorway? How would you have felt if you had?'

Only now do I think I begin to realise what she is asking, and, after a few more moments considering it, I do my best to put it into words.

'Well, if when I opened the door in the tree I had seen the house, I don't think I would even have stepped through it, so perhaps the walk was necessary so that I allowed this awakening to show me its secrets.'

I look to Ruby for confirmation and can see that my response is what she had been hoping to hear.

'That is true Ruby; these awakenings are for your benefit. They will provide the answers that you seek, but you have to allow them too. They are all part of your story and until you have seen all they have to show you, and understood at least most of them, the biggest truth you seek cannot be made known to you. It is for this reason you must always keep moving forward. So, shall we try and work out another piece of this latest puzzle?'

I don't know why, but I am crying now, however, for the first time I really begin to feel as though I am making some important connections.

'Yes Elsie, I would like to at least try to understand part of this awakening.'

'Alright child, your fear when the house first came into view was all consuming and you froze. It was at this point you became aware that you were not alone and called out to me. I could not answer you with words then, as you had another important lesson to learn, can you think what that might have been?'

'Do you mean when the lions caught me as I fell, Elsie?'

She does not answer, but her expression tells me to continue exploring this thought.

'When I fell I was expecting to fall onto hard, sharp stones and for it to be painful, but the velvet paws of those great creatures saved me from being hurt, and I felt so safe and secure that I wanted to stay right there, although I knew I couldn't. I was glad I had not seen them first or I would have been sure to try and get away from them. But they looked after me, protected me, and something tells me that even if I had seen them and moved away, their great paws would still have caught me. I think perhaps I needed to know that just because something appears to be wrong or painful or uncomfortable, it may be there to help, support and guide me to where I need to be. I don't think the lions were there to harm me but to protect and help me. I think that I was being told that if I am where I need to be, then no harm will come to me.'

Looking at Elsie, I can see by the tears in her eyes that all I have said is what she has been longing to hear.

'Oh dearest Ruby, you have learnt two very important lessons today and with that knowledge you will begin to discover more and more. It does not mean that you will never feel frightened or anxious, but it does mean that you will be able to use your new found knowledge to help you through all that may be ahead of you. Are you alright child, do you want to stop?'

I am tired, and part of me wants to stop, but a greater part wants to learn as much as I can. I really feel that this is a turning point for me, and soon I will have all the answers I could possibly want.

'Please Elsie, I think I would like to try and unravel a little more.'

'Very well Ruby, but if I think I have had enough, I will stop. You cannot cope with too much all at once. I think too much of you to allow you to push yourself too

hard, do you understand Ruby?'
My mind flashes back to the message I was reading this morning and its very last line.

> *'But rest assured you'll always be,*
> *The one who means the most to me.*

Feeling encouraged, I decide to ask Elsie what it means. But as I do her face changes.

'Alas Ruby, I dearly wish I could tell you everything, you have come so far today, but that mystery is for another time.'

She looks away as if trying to hide her true feelings from me. Now I feel guilty and wish I had never asked that question.

'Oh Elsie, I did not mean to hurt or upset you, please forgive me, we can stop if you want to?'

'Dearest Ruby, there is nothing to forgive child, you have not hurt or upset me and of course we can continue, at least for a little while. It is just that, as I have often told you, the truth will change everything for both of us, so that can only happen at the right time.' Now, what would you like to unravel next Ruby?'

I sit and think through all I have seen for several minutes before answering Elsie. When I do, I can see from the look on Elsie's face my response surprises, yet thrills her at the same time.

'Please Elsie; I would like to know more about my Uncle. Today I have seen him as a baby and as a child; I also saw you and can see now that your link with my Aunt and Uncle goes back much further than I first realised. I have always been so fearful of both of them, but today the things I have seen begin to make me feel sorry for my Uncle. I also feel much more confused than before about the vast difference in ages between them. Can you help me to understand at least some of what I have seen?'

'Well Ruby, I can certainly try, why don't you start with the first time you saw him?'

'Well, the first time I saw him was when I found myself in a very grand-looking nursery surrounded by so many beautiful toys, the likes of which I had never seen before. In fact, I didn't so much see him as I did hear him to begin with. He was tucked away in a baby's cot and sobbing bitterly. When I first heard him I was really irritated, but when I saw him and continued to watch as a stern, sharp-featured woman snatched him up so harshly and left with no love for him, my heart melted and I found myself close to tears. Then the scene changed and all the toys had been replaced by…'

'Let's stop there Ruby, we need to take each scene separately. Before we begin to unravel this part, can I ask why you were so irritated by his crying?'

'I…I think perhaps part of me was jealous of the things which surrounded him, I felt as though a child who had been given so much should be happy, and that there was no reason for such anguish in one so young. Was I wrong Elsie?'

Elsie sits and smiles at me as though she knows exactly how I had felt.

'Well now Ruby, I can see exactly why you thought the way you did, but you need to remember that just because somebody appears to have everything, they may be lacking the most important thing of all. You know only too well what it is like not to be loved, don't you? Mere things can never replace this most important need of all can they?'

Elsie was right, until I came to the Manor; I had never really known what real love was. It is true that I had often thought I wanted toys and belongings, but since coming here with nothing, I have been given everything I needed and yet I still own very little.

My reply is croaky and strained as I think about all that Elsie has just said.

'I yearned for so long to be loved and wanted, that I began to think owning things was what it was all about, but now I know I couldn't have been more wrong. Was my Uncle never wanted or loved? The lady who took him from the cot certainly did appeared not to have any sort of feeling or concern for him at all.'

'You are right in all you have said about her Ruby, she was only employed as a nurse and governess to him and grudged being given such a young charge. But to say he was never loved or wanted simply isn't true. Your Uncle was born into the most loving family any child could wish for, but tragedy followed almost immediately when his devoted mother became ill and died within weeks of his birth. His father was so broken by the loss of his wife that he began to resent his baby son so much that he blamed him for the loss of his wife. So, the lady you saw was employed to care for him out of the sight of his father. As your Uncle got older his father did begin to soften towards him, but sadly tragedy was just around the corner and he too died before your Uncle reached his fourth birthday. The only family he had left were a Great Aunt and Uncle who had always wanted to live in that house, but already had a daughter who was a good deal older than your Uncle was. They only agreed to care for him out of duty and to get their hands on that house. But, very soon their daughter found herself looking after him. She quickly grew to resent him and her parents for this, but knew he was her only chance of continuing to live the life she now thought herself entitled too. Despite her resentment, she soon learnt that his placid nature allowed her to dominate him, she started to enjoy this and her new found power.'

Elsie stops, and looking at me, can see that I am feeling every part of this story very deeply indeed.

'Ruby, I think we should stop child, your distress is already obvious and I am afraid it may only increase.'

'Oh Elsie, please, can we not finish at least this part today?'

Elsie pauses, her look of concern for me is only too evident in her gentle face. Trying hard to calm myself, I repeat my question. Eventually Elsie gives in and continues.

'Very well, but only to the end of this part of the story.'

'Thank you Elsie, this is so important to

me. Before you go on, may I ask a question, please?'

'You can, but I think you have already worked the answer out for yourself haven't you?'

'Well, I'm not sure; I could give it a try. The girl I saw in the second part, which I recognised as my Aunt, is that this daughter? If so, why does she still have such a hold over him, and why did I see you with her as a child?'

'I knew you had worked some of it out for yourself, yes, she is indeed the lady you have always known as your Aunt, and yes, she is that daughter. But, as for my presence there, that is for another time. The hold she has over him is one that is driven by his own fear. She is the only real security he has ever known, and now he is so dependent upon her because she has convinced him that he will not cope without her.'

'Why Elsie, why would she do that to him? Why would she do that to any close relative?'

'Her reasons are purely selfish Ruby, she is only too aware that her ability to remain at your Uncle's house, and live the life to which she has become so accustomed, is only possible while your Uncle allows it. If ever he decided to marry…'

Elsie stops abruptly, almost as though she is unable to continue, with a look on her face of such melancholy that I fear she may soon be in tears herself. However, she soon forces herself to regain her composure and continues.

'Oh sorry Ruby, don't mind me, where was I? Ah yes, if he ever decided he no longer needed or wanted her with him, she would have nowhere to go. The reality of this sad situation is that she is actually far more insecure than he is, unfortunately he is unable or unwilling to see this, so the isolation for him continues.'

'That is so cruel, she is just horrible! My Uncle has always seemed afraid of her, even when I was living there, now I know why.'

'Oh Ruby, he is not so much afraid of her, as afraid of what his life could have been, nay, could still be without her. As I have already said, he never really knew either of his parents, so when he found himself faced with… No, we'll not go there today, but Ruby, please do not think too harshly of your Aunt either, she is not altogether to blame for her attitude or her behaviour. Her childhood was not as happy as it could have been either.'

An uneasy silence now fills the room and surrounds us both. I feel unable to break it, and for whatever reason, Elsie seems unwilling too either. She appears lost in her own thoughts, almost dreaming.   I feel she may even be wishing for something which might have been, now out of reach. However, after several minutes I manage to find the courage once more to speak, and I ask the question which has been burning in me to ask.

'What was it you stopped yourself from saying earlier, and why were you here as a child Elsie?'

A look of something resembling terror flashes across her face, and I realise that my question was one that Elsie has been dreading. As she answers, the tremor in her voice is very evident and I fear now what is to follow.

'Ruby, have you not guessed at least some of the answer to that question? I fear I may have said too much already.'

An icy shiver runs right through me before I feel hot and unsteady and my head begins to spin so violently, as thoughts which fill me with horror begin swirling round in my mind.

'Oh Elsie, I am too afraid to even tell you the thoughts flooding my mind at the moment. If I am wrong my heart may break again, and if I am right, oh what if I am right? I don't know what to do!'

Unable to speak anymore, my voice gives way to tears as Elsie moves over to stand at my side.

'Dear Ruby, you must tell me what you think you know child, or you will be in torment until you do.'

'But Elsie…'

'Take it slowly. You can do it, I know you can.'

'When you stopped yourself saying something, Elsie, I didn't understand why, or what it was, but now I can only see one thing it could be. You stopped before telling me that my Uncle is really my father didn't you?'

Even as the words leave my mouth, I can see by Elsie's reaction that I am right.

'Does that mean my Aunt is my real mother?'

A look of something resembling relief floods across Elsie's panicked face.

'No Child, she is not, but the rest is as you say.'

'I think I would like to stop now Elsie, I don't want to know anymore. I can hardly believe that my father is alive after all these years believing I was an orphan.'

The Diary of Miss Ruby March

A single tear escapes from Elsie's eyes before she can stop it, but I dare not ask her why, not now.

'Dearest Ruby, you have discovered a lot today, and you need time to think and work things out. I too think you should return to the Manor. When you are ready I will accompany you as far as the steps up to the main door.'

'I…I didn't mean I wanted to go, just to stop unravelling things. Please don't make me go back yet.'

After a short pause, I know I need to ask one more question which could bring an answer I dread more than any I have received yet.

'Elsie, does he know who I really am, and if he does, why does he not love me?'

'Oh Ruby, he does know and he does love you. You must believe this, but remember what I told you. He is afraid of being hurt and does not really know how he should feel or react as he has never had an example to follow.'

My response is one of disbelief.

'I know, it is just that I never thought I would know anyone related to me, especially either of my parents.'

'Ruby, I cannot tell you how wrong

you still are, but know this;

A memory is all they have of you,
But soon a chance to make things new,
A life for all can yet begin,
Just open your heart and let them in.

That is all you have to do sweet Ruby, but the time must be right and there is more you need you know. Just wait and be patient for a little while longer, things will change, I promise.'

'That poem is beautiful Elsie, but what does it mean?'

'For now dearest child, just read it, believe it and trust in it. The time has come now for you to return to the Manor, but this may not be for long.'

No more words pass between us, but Elsie opens the door to her cottage and before we have taken two steps, the door to the Manor appears in front of us. I turn to say goodbye, but Elsie and her cottage have gone. I enter the Manor but know that my time here may now be coming to an end.

The Diary of Miss Ruby March

15 July 1877

The long hot days of summer should fill me with joy and blissful serenity, but ever since the last awakening, less than a week ago, my mood has been one of melancholy and utter bewilderment. This morning is no exception. As I try to hide my true feelings from Miss Florence, I can see that she is beginning to become suspicious.

'Oh Ruby, why are you so quiet? We don't have nearly so much fun as we used too. Can we please go to the woods? They are so beautiful this time of year and the trees are great to hide behind, and even inside sometimes.'

The woods is the last place I feel like going, especially today, as I cannot help feeling that there is where the next awakening will be, and soon. Miss Florence must not be with me when this happens, but how can I stop her without telling her everything? What can I do? Oh Elsie, please help me!

'What was that? Who is Elsie?'

I realise I am thinking out loud, and Miss Florence is not the type of person who will accept anything other than a believable truth, however untrue that truth turns out to be.

'Oh Miss Florence I did not realise I

was talking so loudly. You know how much I love to write stories don't you? Well, Elsie is a character in one of them.'

Miss Florence makes no reply, but I can see from her expression that she is not at all convinced by my explanation.

Our walk continues, and by now it is clear we are indeed heading towards the woods. I can feel my heart thumping the closer I get to the little wooden door, but to my relief, before opening it Miss Florence stops once more and stands facing me with what can only be described as an extremely determined expression on her face.

'Goodness, Miss Florence, what an expression. Whatever is the matter now?'

'Well, I don't believe you, I like writing stories too, but I don't ask any of my characters for help. I think it is far more likely to be something to do with your early morning walks, the ones when you leave me behind.'

Feeling the heat creeping up my neck and face, I turn away and attempt to change the subject. However, Miss Florence is in full flow now and not to be stopped.

'I think you are meeting someone in secret on these mornings, and I don't believe their name is Elsie. I think you've got a secret sweetheart and you are afraid of getting caught, that's why you said Elsie. I am right aren't I? See, you're blushing so it must be true.'

I knew Miss Florence had a vivid imagination, but I would never have thought her capable of such an elaborate storyline. Now, in spite of myself and my fear, I find myself unable to prevent my amusement from showing, and I begin to giggle quite uncontrollably.

'What is so funny? Why are you laughing Ruby? Father always says that giggles are a nervous reaction and used to cover up something we are embarrassed about! Therefore, I can only assume I am correct, and that you have been found out! Come on, I have no wish to go to the woods now, I want to go to the turret room.'

As she flounces off back towards the Manor my relief turns to panic as the reality of what she has just said sinks in, she said the turret room. I have promised not to enter that place, but must not let her see my reluctance this time. So, in the brightest tone I can manage, I call after her.

'Well, if that is what you believe then it has to be true. But, I think the turret room will have to wait as it is nearly lunchtime.'

The Diary of Miss Ruby March

By the time I have caught up with a very smug, self-satisfied Miss Florence, we have already reached the main door.

'I'm starving Ruby, I hope lunch is ready, I could eat a whole banquet right now.'

'I thought you wanted to visit the turret room?'

My reply is teasing and flippant, but came out of immense relief.

'Oh I can go there anytime, after lunch I think we should both write a story and then ask father and mother to choose the best one.'

'Do you think that is a good idea Miss Florence? I'm not at all sure your parents will approve of such hard fought competition.'

This is said purely in jest as I know that Lord and Lady Haskell will be highly amused by such an idea, but Miss Florence takes it seriously as always.

'They must approve, it is what I want to do, and you must convince them Ruby.'

'Oh Miss Florence, I think they will take it much better if the idea comes from you. Why don't you ask them over lunch?'

'I will, and then they cannot refuse, because you can say you want to do it too. They like you and will never refuse.'

I smile to myself as I try and imagine the somewhat one-sided conversation which is about to happen, and the mock protestations from Lord Haskell himself. Although deep down I know that as soon as I can this afternoon I must escape and make for the woods alone. The next awakening is waiting for me there, and I know it is coming today.

I was quite correct about the Lord and Lady's response and amusement, although Miss Florence becomes quite indignant and eventually demands to be taken seriously. I can see that her parents, particularly her father, has great difficulty in trying to suppress his amusement; however, after a short while something resembling order is restored. Lord Haskell also agrees to read both stories, although he stops short of agreeing to choose a favourite. Miss Florence endeavours to make him change his mind, but she soon realises that further protestations in this direction are useless. Once her father has made a decision she knows there is very little chance of him changing his mind.

As soon as lunch is over Miss Florence glances impatiently at me and leaves the table. Hoping she may go on without me, I remain seated; however, my hopes of this are soon shattered, and reluctantly I leave my seat and join her in the doorway fleetingly, before I find myself being dragged up the stairs to her room.

'Miss Florence, don't you think we should write our stories in our own rooms if they are to be judged by your father?'

'You heard him Ruby; he said he is prepared to read them, but not to pick a favourite. This being the case, if we write in the same room and help each other it doesn't matter does it?'

Once again I find myself caught out, and can think of no way out. Feeling somewhat despondent, and more than a little ashamed at my lack of ability to counteract Miss Florence's reasoning, I allow myself to be led to her room. Taking a seat in the window, while she positions herself at her neat white-painted desk, I fear that my escape will not come. So, accepting the paper and writing utensils which have been thrust at me, I start to write. To begin with I feel void of any inspiration, but I soon find myself writing easily, and quite enjoying it too. The most surprising thing to me is the fact that Miss Florence remains fixed on the task, silent and unmoving for a whole hour before even looking up.

'How are you getting on Miss Florence?'

'Ssh, I can't talk to you now Ruby, I am

far too busy writing.'

Unable to stop myself I giggle under my breath, almost choking myself as I attempt not to be heard. I know now that the awakening will have to wait, at least until Miss Florence's aunt arrives to take tea with her sister and niece at around half past four. This time is always my own, and I should be able to make my escape then.

My writing continues to flow easily and by the time I hear the clock strike four downstairs in the hallway I have written quite a lengthy tale, and feel quite pleased with it. I look up to find Miss Florence still hard at work. If I knew this was all it took to keep her still and quiet I would have suggested it myself weeks ago.

'Miss Florence, have you nearly finished? Your poor father will be reading all night, and you need to change and be ready to take tea with your aunt when she arrives.'

'Oh, I had forgotten that, alright I am nearly finished anyway. Cam you read it for me while I get ready? I don't want to give it to father before you've seen it, I need to know it is not just rubbish.'

'Miss Florence, I am sure it is not rubbish, and I know your father will enjoy it immensely. But if it pleases you I would love to read it.'

It is only now that I see how much there is to read, and my heart sinks once more. If I read all this I will never get away, perhaps that is what Miss Florence is hoping.

'I will try and read it all, but you have written so much that I may have to finish it another time.'

As soon as these words leave my mouth I know I have made a mistake.

'Why Ruby, it isn't as though you have anything else to do this afternoon is it?'

The smugness in her voice makes me resent her a little, but I also know that if she doesn't know, how can she possibly understand? Before I can respond to her, the doorbell can be heard ringing, indicating the arrival of her aunt.

'Oh bother, I have to go now, you will read it won't you, please say you will?'

'Of course, now I will get into trouble if you are late, be off with you'

Her request this time was much more heartfelt, almost pleading in its nature, and as she leaves I decide to at least read a page or two, but not until I get back. Time here at the Manor stands till anyway during an awakening, so I should have plenty of time before she returns.

I wait to leave her room until I hear the door of the parlour close below me, and then as silently as possible I descend the stairs and make my way outside. The cool late afternoon breeze is both refreshing and comforting as I make my way through the walled garden towards the door which filled me with such fear only this morning. However, this afternoon that fear is not as intense, in fact it has all but completely disappeared. I open the small wooden door and almost as soon as I step through it, I know that the wood I am standing in is different from the one I have always found myself in before. It almost feels enchanted in some way.

The steps down from the doorway appear to be the same, but everything else seems to be hanging in a state of suspended trance-like expectancy, as though stuck in a time frame long passed, unable to escape its strange entrapment.

As I reach the bottom of the steps I stop. Hardly able to breathe I begin to realise that I have seen and experienced a similar thing before, only that time it seemed to herald the beginning of winter. I have gone back. Back to the place, and time of my very first awakening, only now I am sure I will find out more, and maybe Elsie will join me here. No sooner has this thought entered my head, Elsie is at my side.

'Are you ready Ruby?'

'Oh Elsie, I am so glad you are here, but ready for what?'

'Come, follow me and you will see all the things that you didn't see before, and just maybe put some more pieces of that puzzle together.'

No further words are spoken, but I feel glad to have Elsie at my side. I am still nervous at what I might witness, I also feel glad to be back here. I might actually discover the end to the story, the first story I wrote when I came here, and when the awakenings first began.

As we approach the area of the Dragon and the Maiden, I begin to wish that I had thought to bring my notebooks with me. But then why would I? How could I have known what I was going to witness this afternoon? I couldn't, but I do know that upon my return to the Manor I must find this story, and record all that I am about to see, and finish this tale properly.

Upon reaching the exact same spot where I had stood all those months before, Elsie stops so abruptly that I nearly walk into her.

'Oh, oh sorry Elsie I was away with my thoughts and memories of the first time I was here, I didn't notice that you had stopped. This is exactly…'

Elsie says nothing, but her smile tells me that now is not a time for words. I turn and look towards the Dragon seeing immediately that the huge yellow eye is already open and staring, only this time he does appear to see us. He begins to raise his great head and body from its resting place, and this time it is he that moves towards the maiden. She appears to still be sleeping and unaware of his efforts to wake her, but as I look more closely I can see that her eyes too are open. I want to ask Elsie why she does not respond to the Dragon, but know that now is a time for silence and respect, not for words and questions.

As we continue to stand there, and with a tremendous shuddering jolt, everything around us begins to swirl violently and change. The strangest part of all is that Elsie and I remain still and untouched by this dramatic eruption. We appear to be part of it, yet somehow separate. Then, as abruptly as it had begun, everything is calm and peaceful once more. As I look to where the dragon and maiden had been, I see instead a young couple wrapped in each other's embrace so tightly that anyone would think their very lives depended on never letting go. As I continue to watch, I can see that she is barely as old as I am now, and he not much older. Who are they? What is it about them I find so familiar?

Eventually the figures part just enough to allow me to see their faces clearly for the first time. I gasp. For there, standing in front of me are, Elsie and Master Edward, or at least I think that's who they are. But there is something about Master Edward that doesn't seem quite right. Master Edward is at least eight years younger than Elsie, so it can't be him, yet the resemblance is uncanny.

Elsie sees my confusion, and although we continue to watch in silence, she takes my hand and smiles. The scene begins to change again, and now the only figure I can see is the one that looks like Elsie, and she is crying. In the distance a horse-drawn carriage disappears behind the horizon and I know instantly that the young man is on board, never to return. It is only as I look at Elsie standing beside me, that I realise my vision has become obscured by hot salty tears.

'Come Ruby, we must move on now. Our time today is short, and there is something else you must see.'

As we turn to retrace our steps and leave the wood, the Dragon and the Maiden are once more where they have always been, but as we pass by a single tear again falls from the great yellow eye as it closes once more. This time it almost feels as though it is closing for good, never again to open. At this thought a lump forms in my throat, I wish more than anything else in the world right now I could heal these two broken hearts and lives.

As we climb the few steps up to the small wooden door, I am relieved at the thought of once more being in the pretty walled garden, but cannot resist the temptation to take another glance at the Dragon. As I do so, his expression appears to changes from one of forlornness and heartfelt longing to one of blissful peace and contentment, in fact he almost appears to be smiling, but how and why? What can have changed? We pass through the little wooden door and my initial relief is short-lived, as what lies on the other side is not the walled garden of the Manor, but, a bustling London street with large imposing white town houses on both sides. Unable to remain silent any longer, I ask Elsie why we are here.

'We are here because you need to know

the end of the story. Come with me, there is nothing for you to fear child.'

Feeling anxious and uncertain I follow Elsie, until we come to the door of one of these impressive houses. Knowing that our next steps will take us inside my heart begins to thump harder, my mouth is dry too, making it hard for me to swallow or even breathe. As we enter, I am surprised by how bright and airy it is, however, the atmosphere is one I know only too well. It is stifling and severe. I feel this even before I see anyone, and it is only reinforced when I do. We move briskly along the tiled hallway and towards the very grand imposing staircase at the far end. Even before we begin to climb I can hear someone crying bitterly. This time it sounds like the sobs of a young man, this immediately makes me feel even more uncomfortable as I am not used to hearing men or boys of any age cry. I say nothing, and continue to silently follow Elsie.

Halfway up the stairs and at the point where the staircase changes direction, Elsie stops and turns to look at me. Her expression, as always is kind and warm, only this time there is a seriousness about it that I have not seen before.

'Elsie, are you alright? What is it? I

have not seen you look like this before.'

'Dear, sweet Ruby, you remember me telling you not to enter the turret room don't you?'

'Of course Elsie, and I have kept my promise to you. But what has that got to do with this house, I don't understand?'

'Hush child, I know you have kept your promise and of course you don't understand, but before we go on there is something I have to explain to you alright?'

I say nothing, but nod my head and wait for her to continue, while all the time my uneasiness and hatred of this place continues to build.

'Ruby, earlier this afternoon you saw two young people who I know you felt you recognised as myself and Master Edward, although this confused you because of the difference in our ages. Well, the people who you saw were not who you thought them to be. They were, however, people you need to know about, as they are part of your story and part of the secret contained in the turret room.'

Elsie pauses as she breathes in deeply as though trying to find the right words to use. I say nothing, I am trying hard to fight the almost overwhelming feeling of the need to escape this place and see and hear no more, but I know that Elsie would not show or tell me anything that I do not need to know, or that would do me any harm. Eventually the uncomfortable silence ends as Elsie continues.

'The two young people you saw Ruby lived many years ago and are where your story begins. His name was Frederick and hers was May. As you saw earlier they were very much in love although they were not much older than you are now. However, Frederick's parents did not approve of their relationship so insisted he move to London and live with his Aunt and Uncle. They also wanted him to be educated there, and later trained in a respectable profession. His departure left both himself and May heartbroken, until a change in the fortune of May's parents brought them also to London. This change could have been devastating for all of them, as they lost everything and had to move in with May's Great Aunt, but for the young May this was the best thing that could have happened.

May's Great Aunt was not an easy lady to live with, although she saw in May something of her own young self and these two unlikely people began to form a close bond. For the first time, May had found someone she could truly confide in about her heartbreaking love story that had been so cruelly cut short. Her Great Aunt listened intently and with great sympathy, as unbeknown to May, she had suffered in an almost identical way, which is why she had never married. This also went someway to explaining her, at times bitter and sharp personality.

By the time May had finished telling her story, her Great Aunt had already decided that she was not going to let May suffer the same fate as herself. She was well known and respected in polite society, and not without influence. She made up her mind to do everything in her power to reunite the two young lovers, and thus, heal their hearts, and right what in her eyes was a vicious and malicious wrong. We are here today Ruby so you can see that reunion and something of what followed for yourself.'

Unable to speak, and with my vision distinctly hazy once more, I wait for Elsie to either continue climbing the stairs, or with her story, but she does neither.

After another, even more uncomfortable, silence it is I who regains the ability to speak.

'Oh Elsie, I still don't understand what any of this has to do with me? Please don't leave me here alone; you will stay with me won't you?'

'I will wait here for you child, you must see the next part without me, as I need you to watch without distraction, and then we will talk and see if you can find a connection to your own story.'

'But how do I know where to go? What if I find...'

'Hush now, your guide for this next part has just arrived.'

Before I can ask what she means or who it is, I hear the great front door open once again and through it walks May herself, but now she looks less like Elsie and more like, no it can't be. But it is, or at least appears to be, Elsie's mother now walking up the stairs towards me.

'Don't be frightened Ruby, May is expecting you, go with her now child.'

The delicate figure coming towards me smiles and holds out her hand, with one final glance towards Elsie I know I am safe.

'Come Ruby, come with me now and I pray you will begin to understand a little more, and answer some more of those questions.'

I say nothing, but am beginning to feel that what I am about to see and what will follow is going to change my life completely. This thought scares me, and I really don't know if I am ready for it, or even want it, but knowing Elsie wants it for me is enough to keep me going.

Obediently I follow May as she climbs the remaining stairs. She makes her way along a corridor towards a door at the far end. We stop just before reaching it, and May appears to be calming herself before facing what lies beyond.

'Are you ready, Ruby?'

'Ready for what, Miss May?'

'Please, just call me Gr… Just call me May.'

Her sudden correction confuses me. What was she going to say before she stopped herself? What do I need to be ready for?

'Please May; what do I need to be ready for?'

'Oh, I'm sorry Ruby, are you ready to see this part of your story?'

'I…I don't know, I know Elsie wants me too, but I am afraid of what I might see.'

'Dear Ruby, you must understand that what you will see cannot hurt you, only explain, I hope, more of your story child.'

We slowly approach the door and May reaches for the handle, but then stops herself, and I begin to wonder whether she is ready to face whatever lies beyond it. Then with a slow, very deep breath and a new look of, what can only be described as determination, not only on her face, but displayed by her whole body, she turns the handle. Nothing could prepare me for the sight that greets my eyes.

I was expecting a grand, light and airy room, but despite its grandeur, it is almost dark and quite stifling as we enter. It is only after my eyes adjust to the gloom that I realise the windows are closed and curtains drawn. The reason for this soon becomes clear, and I cannot help but gasp, as I see in the bed before me the young man who was so in love with May, so thin and gaunt he is almost unrecognisable. I shiver, wondering if he is dead. However, upon hearing us approach the foot of his bed, his dark eyes open, and for what must have been the first time in a very long while, his thin lips form a weak but heartfelt smile.

'May, my darling, May! Is that really you? I can scarcely believe my eyes. Oh, how I have longed for this day, but...'
May's reply falters with emotion as the words pas her quivering lips.

'But what my sweetest Frederick?'
'But... but you should not have to see

me like this, our reunion should be joyous
and full of life, not born out of sickness and
filled with sadness and pity.'

As I stand beside May I can see her
struggling to remain in control of her
emotions, I soon become aware that I have
already lost my own battle and tears fall
freely down my cheeks. I am relieved that
Frederick does not appear to be aware of my
presence, and even May now seems to no
longer see me. Maybe I could, or perhaps
should, just creep out and return to Elsie. But
then, Elsie wants me to be here. Oh, what
should I do?

I turn to look back at the door through
which we entered only a few moments ago.
Although I know we left it open it is now
closed, and something about it, and indeed
this whole room, seems different. Something
is changing here but I don't know what. I
turn back towards the touching scene of May
and Frederick once more. May is now sitting
on the bed holding Frederick's thin pale hand
with such tenderness; my vision becomes
even more blurred.

'Ruby, come here child, sit beside me
will you?'

I desperately try to think of an excuse why
I should not, but soon find myself doing

exactly as May asks me to do. The lump in my throat is making it hard to swallow, let alone talk, and yet I know there is something I have to ask, but should I ask May or wait and ask Elsie later?

After a short while, I decide I cannot wait any longer, so take a deep breath and ask May.

'Please May, is Frederick … is he dead?'
May looks at me with an expression I have only ever seen in Elsie before, taking my hand in hers, she answers in little more than a whisper.

'No Ruby, he is not dead child, merely sleeping, but he is gravely ill. I cannot say more to you at present without telling you a truth which you need to hear from someone else. But know this; if he was to die now, your story could not start.'

I do not understand what this means, but again a shudder runs right through me and my head begins to whirl with such violence that I fear I may pass out altogether.

As May and I continue to sit side by side on the edge of Frederick's bed, the dim light appears to be getting dimmer, and soon the room is almost completely enveloped in darkness. I find myself moving even closer to

May as the whole atmosphere becomes thick and oppressive. May has told me that he is not dead, and has also led me to believe that he is not going to die, as this would prevent my story from even beginning. What does all this mean? Is May really Elsie's own dear mother? If she is, how could Frederick be her father when he looks nothing like I have seen him before? Once more my mind goes back to the words May stopped herself from saying. What was it about that minute which had made me shudder like that? What couldn't she tell me just a few moments ago? I can feel myself trembling all over, before a comforting arm pulls me close.

'Hush Ruby, do not distress yourself so, bringing you here was only meant to help you to understand and to learn more of your story. I think perhaps you have seen enough for today, although...'

May pauses, causing me to open my tear-filled eyes and gaze in the flickering light of a single candle, into her gentle, kind face.

'Although what?'

My voice is little more than a husky whisper.

'Ruby, do you think you could bear to remain here for just a short while longer so that this part of your story at least is known to you, even if not fully understood as yet?'

'I...I don't know, but I will try, I just wish it wasn't so dark and stuffy in here.'

May says nothing, but in the same weak flickering candlelight her sweet mouth forms into a smile.

I think I must have fallen asleep, because as I open my eyes this time the oppressive, choking atmosphere has gone, and sunlight is streaming through the now open, window. As my eyes begin to adjust once more, this time to the brightness, I can see that May is no longer sitting beside me, and I begin to panic as I frantically search the vast room for her. It does not take me long to see both herself and Frederick, now looking so much better, and much more like Elsie's own father, sitting together in a large window seat. I make my way over to them, but as I do the door opens and Elsie appears.

'Ruby, it is time to go now child, neither May or Frederick can see us now.'

'So why did I have to stay?'

'You needed to stay so that you could see for yourself that this part of the story at least ended happily, although the years that followed were very much less than kind, but you have seen this for yourself already.'

'I have, when?'

The Diary of Miss Ruby March

We leave the room in silence and make our way back down the stairs, but not to the front door through which we had entered earlier, instead, we make our way behind the staircase and exit through the back door.

I expect to find myself in a garden, but not this garden.

'Oh…oh Elsie, how did we get here?' Turning to look over my shoulder, all I can see is the Manor.

'The awakening is over for today Ruby, our time together is rapidly drawing to a close.'

'But…oh Elsie I have so many questions, so much I need to ask you, none of what I have seen today makes sense, why can I not stay with you longer?'

'Soon child, soon we will meet again, but now is there one question you want to ask before we part?'

Only one, my mind is whirling with so many, how can I choose only one? The one I ask becomes two anyway, causing Elsie some amusement.

'One thing I must know, are May and Frederick your own parents, and if they are, were they the dragon and the maiden?'

With a giggle in her voice Elsie answers.

'Well, I did say one question, but I

think I cannot answer one without the other. Yes Ruby, they are indeed my parents, and yes, you are right, the dragon and the maiden do indeed depict their story. Although, to say they were May and Frederick would not be true. The dragon and the maiden were simply a way of explaining and telling their story. Does this make things clearer child?'

'I think so, but I do wish I could find out more, and I still do not understand the secret held in the turret room. How it can possibly be linked to today?'

I see a flash of panic pass across Elsie's face before she once again makes me repeat my promise not to enter that place.

'I promise Elsie, are you alright? You look frightened.'

'I am just a little tired, you must return now Ruby, but it will not be long before we will be reunited, and then everything will become clear. Take heart child, your waiting will soon be over.

'Please Elsie, when will the next awakening take place?'

'That is your decision Ruby, but remember this;

Search your heart,
Do not fear,

The Diary of Miss Ruby March

Although we now part,
I'll always be near.

Search your heart,
Dry your tears,
A journey must start,
And span the years.

Search your heart,
Do not fear,
We may be apart,
But I'm always here.

Now go, and be prepared to open the next new door.'

I stand at the foot of the steps watching as Elsie walks away, back towards the walled garden. I am still there as the door closes behind her. Then I remember, I promised to read Miss Florence's story. As quickly and silently as I can, I make my way back into the Manor and up to her room. As I enter, I can see by the mantle clock that once again, no time has passed at all, and I begin to read.

I have not read more than a few lines when I hear the door of the parlour below open. Surely Miss Florence has not finished taking tea with her Aunt already? I sit listening intently, but after several seconds with no further sound I assume that it was the tea tray arriving.

By the time Miss Florence does eventually arrive back at her room, I have read all but the last two pages, and am amazed that she allows me to finish without begging me for my opinion. However, the moment I look up and indicate that I have finished, I am bombarded by incessant questioning. I do my best to answer them all, but by the time we have to go down for dinner, I am already exhausted and cannot help feeling sorry for Lord Haskell, as he is forced to read two stories by two young girls immediately following dinner this evening.

The Diary of Miss Ruby March

7 August 1877

Days have passed since the day of the story writing, and although Lord Haskell did read them both that evening, he had told his persistently questioning daughter that he needed more time to read them again before he could choose his favourite. This had frustrated her greatly, but I have watched while he read them and could see that they both moved him greatly, and as he came to the end of mine he had looked towards me with a look of knowing and understanding. This had surprised me, and ever since I had wanted to ask him about it. However, the right opportunity has not presented itself, until now that is.

This morning Miss Florence had woken me even earlier than usual, by knocking on my door. To begin with I had thought that there must be something very wrong, and was more than a little annoyed when all she had to tell me was after breakfast her mother wanted to spend some time with her. She did not seem very pleased by this, but it did mean that at least for a while, my time was going to be my own.

After finally persuading her that wandering around in one's night attire was not acceptable behaviour for young ladies, I had climbed back into my own bed hoping to get a little more sleep. Unfortunately, it soon became apparent that this was not going to happen. I was now wide awake and still a little frustrated about being woken so early. So, I got up and dressed hoping to walk for a while in the gardens, but as I looked out of the window, I could rain falling steadily, so decided instead to write something. Having sat staring at the blank page with nothing coming to me for what seemed to be hours, I was relieved to finally be able to make my way down to breakfast. I had already decided that when breakfast was over I was going to ask Lord Haskell if I may speak with him, but as I begin to descend the stairs I feel my confidence is waning and in tatters.

All of a sudden I am back in my last place of torture, feeling as I did when facing the Matron for committing one misdeed or another. Although I had only left there a year ago, and in spite of returning during some of the awakenings, until now it had seemed like a lifetime away. But now, it was as real as it ever had been.

Why was I feeling like this? Lord Haskell had never been anything but loving and kind towards me, almost treating me like his own daughter.

'His own daughter.'

That last thought hangs over me and I shudder. Shaking myself back to reality, I tell myself that I am being ridiculous, and that scenario makes no sense, as I have already discovered that, to my horror, the man I had always thought to be my Uncle is in fact my father, and yet something here makes no sense. Then the words of Matron start ringing in my ears;

'Girls like you need to learn their place.'

By the time I reach the dining room I have decided that I have no right to ask to speak with Lord Haskell at all, and that I will just have to accept that I will never know what his look that night had meant. As I enter the dining room and make my way to my usual seat, trying not to make eye contact with anyone, particularly Lord Haskell, something happens that I have dreaded more than any other.

Lord Haskell speaks to me.

'Ruby, would you please meet with me in my study after breakfast child, there is something of great importance which I must share and discuss with you urgently.'

My heart begins to pound; chest tightens, head whirls and my throat feels as though it is closing. This is it, this is the time I had feared the most, I am going to be asked to leave and not return. Trying my hardest not to let my feelings show, I agree and take my place at the table, but by now the thought of food is almost more than I can bear.

I eventually manage to force myself to swallow some toast for appearances sake, and I sit until everyone else has finished. Everything in me is telling me to make my excuses and leave, but I fight to remain in my seat, knowing that as my employer, it is my duty to adhere to Lord Haskell's request. It is as I sit here; I see Miss Florence and her mother tell each other with their eyes that it is time to leave.

This was planned, Miss Florence knew her father wanted to see me, how much does she know? What has she told him? I can feel my neck and face begin to burn and I know, my now rosy, not to say florid complexion, is giving away my feelings of embarrassment and terror. However, the family are far too polite to say anything.

As the door closes, Lord Haskell rises from

his chair at the head of the table and makes his way to my side.

'Come Ruby, there is much we need to talk about and, knowing how impatient my daughter is, our time is probably short.'

The rich, deep, kindly voice of this very gentle man would usually calm me, but this morning nothing feels the same. Everything feels as though it is changing, falling apart, and I am not ready to lose this haven of safety and love yet. However, still hearing Matron's words in my head, I obey his request without question.

I have only ever set foot in Lord Haskell's study once before, and that was almost a year ago on the day I arrived here, lost, bewildered and very much alone. Now, as I enter this room again, all those same feelings come flooding back as I fear I know what is to come.

Lord Haskell does not take his usual seat behind his desk; instead he makes his way to one of two high-backed, dark green, leather-clad winged armchairs in front of the huge and very ornate fireplace. I stand just inside the door and wait.

'Ruby, are you alright child? Please, come and join me.'

With my legs feeling weak and more than a

little shaky, I slowly make my way across the large room and stand in front of him.

'Sit down child, this is your home, you do not have to wait to be invited to sit here.'

I say nothing but perch myself awkwardly on the edge of the enormous chair. However, almost immediately I feel myself begin to relax. Lord Haskell says nothing straight away, but smiles and then surprises me by leaning forward and clasping his huge hands around my own tiny ones.

'Why Ruby you are trembling child, I do hope you are not frightened of me?'

'No Sir, you have shown me nothing but kindness and love since I arrived here, it is just that…'

I stop myself before I say something which may sound unbelievable to an educated man, such as Lord Haskell. I wonder if I should mention the awakenings or not.

'What is it Ruby? You need keep no secrets from me, with a daughter like mine; there can be nothing I have not already heard.'

'It's nothing Sir; please don't ask me anymore, I fear I could not tell you even if I wanted too.'

'Well, alright we'll leave it for now, although when I have finished talking, I dare say you may have changed your mind. Now, where should I begin? How much do you know already?'

I am already growing increasingly uncomfortable and restless, what does he mean? What does he think I know?

'I think perhaps it would be best to tell you a little about myself, my family and my background to begin with. I guess that you are perhaps curious as to the reason behind us asking you to come here?'

He does not wait for me to answer, but I cannot help feeling he already knows what my answer would be.

'I was born into a large family, the youngest child of eight. Our parents were not wealthy people, and yet they did their very best to ensure we never went without anything. My oldest brother was eleven years old before I came along and it wasn't long before my parents were struggling to cope. By the time I was five years old I had been sent to live with an Aunt and Uncle who had never been blessed with children of their own, and were desperate to have me. I had not wanted to leave all my siblings behind, especially my oldest sister May who, despite being only ten when I was born, had almost taken me on as her own. However, I saw them all often and my remaining childhood was happy and full of love. Then, at the age of twelve, tragedy struck, or so I thought at the time. I was called to Uncle's study and given the worst news I thought I would ever have to hear. My beloved sister, my May, had got married and was expecting a child. I felt as though my whole world was falling apart. My Aunt and Uncle thought I was crying tears of joy, they didn't understand that I feared it would mean she no longer wanted me. But, as time went on, I realised that this could not be further from the truth. As the time for her baby to be born drew nearer, I was sent for. I did not know why, but she had wanted me. So, I left early one spring morning and travelled the many miles to my sister's small but beautiful little cottage.

I was there when my niece was born and remained there for several weeks. I had never felt so special, and when the time came for me to return to the home of my Aunt and Uncle, my sister made me promise to always look after her daughter whatever happened. I did not, could not know, what she meant at the time, but it would only be three short years before I did. It was also at this time I learnt the real meaning of tragedy. Being little more than a child myself, I was not able to honour that promise, and neither were my Aunt and Uncle who, by nothing short of a miracle, had now got their own daughter, who was only two at the time. My heart ached and the guilt I felt was tremendous, however, I vowed that as soon as I was able, I would do everything in my power to right every wrong that had befallen my poor niece, and later her own dear child.

Ruby, do you understand all that I am trying to say to you?'

Unable to answer him, I have sat and listened intently, but with a growing sense of anxiety as the story I am hearing shows such similarity to Elsie's and in parts, my own. It is almost too much to bear.

Finding my voice after several minutes, my response, I know is not what Lord Haskell wants to hear.

'I'm sorry Sir, I'm afraid I don't understand at all. The story you have shared with me is indeed one of tragedy and heartache, but apart from much of it being uncomfortably similar to my own, I can't see any reason for me to hear it.'

A look of panic and almost desperation seems to wash across Lord Haskell's face, before he once again turns to me with his usual kindly smile.

The Diary of Miss Ruby March

'I was afraid that this may be the case, and I am not at liberty to say more, that is at least until…'

'Until what? Oh please Sir, until what?'

A long thoughtful silence passes between us, at least for Lord Haskell it appears to be a thoughtful one, for me it is much more of an awkward, anxious one. Eventually however, Lord Haskell breaks the silence, but does not give me the answers I am so desperately seeking.

'Tell me Ruby, your beautiful, heartfelt story of a few days ago; is it purely a work of fiction, or does it come from a much deeper understanding of things which you have experienced?'

I was most certainly not expecting this. How much does he really know? How much should I tell him? Where should I even begin? The look of terror I am feeling must show on my face as he quickly becomes very concerned.

'Ruby, are you alright child? Have I said something to alarm or distress you? Please, tell me how I may help you?'

' Oh Sir, I am frightened as what I am about to say sounds so bizarre that I am sure you will not believe me, but I do not tell untruths and everything I am about to say really did happen, although when I think about them, they even feel like a dream to me sometimes. I just don't want to displease-'

'Hush child, you will certainly never displease me, and why would I not believe you? Have you been warned in the past for your imagination? I can assure you, that here, you are safe to say anything, and you may be surprised at how believing and accepting I am.'

Although he asked me about being warned for living in my imagination, something inside me makes me feel as though he already knows everything from my past, and even about my future. This makes me shudder, how can this be? However, I begin, shakily at first, to relate everything that I have seen and experienced since my arrival at the Manor one whole year ago.

Lord Haskell listens intently to every minute detail. At several points I am aware that he is drying his eyes with a crisp white linen handkerchief. By the time I reach the end, I know I am safe and have even started to relax a little, although now am exhausted. It is not until Lord Haskell responds, that my anxious fears once again grip me like a vice.

'Thank you Ruby, I know that sharing

all that cannot have been easy for you. But tell me child, having seen and experienced all that you have, how is it that you have still not found the answers you seek? What is holding you back? What is preventing you from believing the truths which lie locked and concealed away in the depth of your heart? Are you still afraid of allowing yourself to be truly happy? Do you really still not know?'

'Oh Sir, what is it that you are asking me? What are you saying? What are the truths which lie locked in my heart? Please won't you tell me, Sir?'

'My sweet child, if only I could, but the ultimate truth is one that you can only discover for yourself. Nobody can tell you what it is, however, I do believe that perhaps you are in need of another awakening, it may not be today, but soon you will once more see things that will undoubtedly make at least some things clearer.

Now child, I am amazed that my daughter has given us so much time, I was certain that by now she-'

Sure enough, before Lord Haskell has finished speaking, an impatient knock is at the door and Miss Florence bounds into the room. Clearing his throat, Lord Haskell attempts to admonish his daughter, but with very little effect.

'Young ladies wait to be invited in after knocking.'

'Sorry Papa, but I was so bored I simply could not wait any longer, you have finished haven't you?'

The second half of her sentence was said with a sudden realisation that just maybe she had interrupted something important.

'As it so happens young lady, we have, but in the future remember to wait before bounding through the door uninvited. It is nearly lunch time, so there will be no going outside until after we have eaten.'

Miss Florence agrees to this without question, although her facial expression undeniably betrays her true feelings in this matter.

The thirty minutes until lunch pass with lightening speed, as I am verbally bombarded by Miss Florence giving me every detail of the time she had spent with her mother. This is fine with me, as I only have to sit and listen, but, I am certain that the endless questions about my morning will come, and soon.

Just for a change lunch is quite a peaceful affair, and on its conclusion I manage to excuse myself and escape to my room without Miss Florence. Her father's request to stay behind and speak with him plays no small part in this, but it is unusual all the same. She protests forcibly, but eventually agrees, and for the first hour of the afternoon I am able to sit alone and recover properly from my emotion-filled morning. By the time my peace is interrupted, I feel fully refreshed and ready to face the inevitable questioning. But, to my surprise, this does not come, and we spend a most pleasant afternoon walking in the gardens with very little chatter passing between us. For the first time I feel as though I am beginning to get to know the real Miss Florence. She is, in fact, not the wild, untamed, excitable puppy she appears to be. But, a well-educated pleasant young girl who only really wants company of her own age.

The Diary of Miss Ruby March

28 September 1877

The reason behind the sudden change in Miss Florence is still not yet clear, but the last few weeks in her company have been delightful. This change has also brought us closer, and helped me not even think about, or wonder, when the next awakening will be. That is, at least, until now. The atmosphere in the garden this afternoon is much the same as it was after I had experienced my very first awakening, and I am feeling uneasy. The leaden grey skies and ever-increasing chill in the air herald the approaching winter, but I know from last year that this will not stop the awakenings. Could this be the awakening that Lord Haskell spoke of? I begin to doubt whether I even want to know all the answers. My biggest fear is that the truth he spoke about, being locked in my heart, what if it being unlocked changes everything? Am I ready for this to happen? Do I even want it too? What if this truth turns out to be a nightmare, instead of a dream? I am so confused, yet if I never find my answers, or unlock this truth, will what I have now last, or just fade away? And if it lasts, will it be enough?

My head is whirling, I am glad to be alone,

at least for a while. Miss Florence is required to take tea with her mother and Aunt again this afternoon, so my time is my own. I continue to wander, but the chill in the air is increasing and I decide to turn to the Manor. I am almost back when the whole atmosphere changes. It becomes still and silent, the chill in the air remains, but something is definitely happening. Nothing has yet made me stop, so upon reaching the steps up to the main door I begin to climb them. It is only as I reach the top and place my hand on the handle of the door that I feel it. The pull to turn and walk back down the steps. Now I know for sure that this is the awakening Lord Haskell had told me to expect.

Slowly I begin to make my way back down the steps, and back towards the walled garden. Why here? I do not know the answer to this, but that is undoubtedly where I am being called too. I arrive at the gate and find it already open with Elsie standing just the other side of it.

'Are you ready Ruby? Our time together today is not long, but following your time spent with Lord Haskell, this extra awakening is necessary to explain a few things.'

'Yes Elsie, I think I am ready, but what

do you mean by 'this extra awakening', was I not supposed to have anymore?'

Elsie does not answer this question, but merely encourages me to step through the gateway and join her. As I do, the scene changes and I find myself watching a young couple, very much in love. The scene is of a wedding, but when the couple turn round, I see whose wedding I am watching. I can scarcely believe it, it is Lord and Lady Haskell. They seem happy, but there is a melancholic feeling surrounding the whole scene. There appear to be no guests, only the minister and three other people in attendance. One is a very fragile-looking lady seated on one side. I gasp, I can see the two others now, I recognise them both instantly as Miss Charlotte and Master Edward.

'Oh Elsie, this makes no sense, how can Miss Charlotte and Master Edward possibly be present at the wedding of their parents? Unless, but that makes even less sense, and who is that other lady, she looks so sad and ill?'

'Hush Ruby, I will answer your questions about today later, but for now we have to watch.'

Elsie and I continue to watch, but now we are viewing a different scene, it is not a wedding this time but a funeral, with Miss Charlotte and Master Edward walking between Lord and Lady Haskell at the front of the very small procession behind the coffin. The lady from the wedding is not present this time, so I can only assume that it is she who has died. The small group appear to turn a corner and then fade from view, but as I look at Elsie I can see my vision is no longer clear and my eyes are stinging with hot salty tears, so I turn away again quickly and unseen. Just then Elsie's voice breaks through the solemn silence.

'Are you ready Ruby? We must leave this place now, there is much to explain and so little time left together today.'

I make no reply but nod my head and follow her out of the walled garden and back towards the Manor. However, the first building my eyes catch sight of is not the Manor, but Elsie's own sweet little cottage. I am relieved to not have to return immediately to the Manor, but I also recall Elsie saying time is short. I never feel as though I have long enough to recover at the cottage, and before I feel ready, I am returning to the Manor and we are separated once more. I realise that each time we meet during an awakening, I find our parting harder and more painful, and my longing to stay is stronger and more palpable.

'Come in child, the fire is lit and the tea is made. Come, sit beside me here.'

The two armchairs which usually sit opposite each other are now side by side facing the warming fire.

'Now, your questions from earlier, what was it that made no sense to you?'

'I was curious how Miss Charlotte and Master Edward could be at their parents wedding?'

Elsie smiled and paused thoughtfully before answering.

'Oh Ruby, dearest Ruby, you asked me once why Lady Haskell still appeared to be so young, well, the awful truth is that Miss Charlotte and Master Edward were born to Lord Haskell's Aunt and Uncle whom he told you about when you met with him. Tragically, following the birth of Master Edward, the then Lord Haskell became very ill and sadly died before his son's first birthday. His dear, devoted wife never really got over the birth of her son as to bear a child, for a lady of her years was not only unusual, but also demanding. The death of her dear husband so soon afterwards proved almost too much for her. She lived until Master

Edward was three years old, and until she had seen her dear nephew married. Once she was happy her children would be taken care of, it was almost as though she eventually allowed herself to join her husband, and she died with all her family at her side. So, you see dear Ruby, Lord and Lady Haskell really are as young as they look, and the reason Lady Haskell was so distressed about Master Edward and Miss Charlotte following the fire, is because she felt as though they had let the children and their parents, particularly their mother down.'

'But why did you tell me they were older siblings of Miss Florence?'

'Did I tell you that child? No, I merely allowed you to believe it until you were able to fully understand this truth. There was much you had to discover before you came to this point. Now, do you have one last question for me before you return to the Manor today?'

I sit and think for several minutes, and then, unaware of where it even comes from, I blurt out a question I didn't even know I had, but am desperate to know the answer to.

'Oh please Elsie, during my meeting with Lord Haskell, he spoke so fondly of his dear sister and her young daughter. It distressed him greatly because he felt that he had failed them both. Please Elsie, are you his niece?'

Elsie pauses, looking almost panicked while she listens to my question, that is until I reach its conclusion, then her usual smile returns and a look of immense relief seems to wash over her.

'Oh Ruby, you are so close now to discovering everything, that I feared you were going to ask me something else, but yes child, Lord Haskell is indeed my Uncle and the dear younger brother of my own dear mother May. Well done dearest Ruby, you have learnt and discovered so much today, but now you must return to the Manor, however, know this;

The secrets which so long have been,
Locked, concealed and hidden,
Will very soon by you be seen,
And known within your heart.

A time is fast approaching,
When what has slept will wake,
When what has been unknown to you,
Will cause new dawns to break.

So do not fear,
Know I am near,

The Diary of Miss Ruby March

The wait is nearly over,
The chains which bind you to the past,
Will very soon be broken.

You will be free,
To live, love and be loved,
Never more to wonder.
The truth you seek,
And yearn to know,
Is just around the corner.

'Oh Elsie, the words are beautiful, but what do they mean?'

'Soon Ruby, soon, but now you must return, do you remember the first time you ever left my cottage?'

'Yes, I do, I simply stepped outside and the Manor appeared!'

'Well, do you want to try again?'

'Must I? Can I not stay here a little longer?'

Elsie makes no reply, but opens the door for me to leave. I glance at her as I pass, and see a single tear making its way slowly down her cheek. She brushes it away quickly, but it was there all the same.

The Manor is once again in front of me and I am barely inside the door before Miss Florence appears, and I find myself being taken into join the other ladies for tea. At first I am more than a little hesitant, but am made to feel so welcome, that I even find myself enjoying their company.

The Diary of Miss Ruby March

6 October 1877

The weather has changed significantly in only a week and it is now obvious that we are going to suffer another harsh, cruel winter, although there is beauty even in this. The first proper fall of snow arrived only yesterday. Now everything is covered in a thick, crystal-encrusted blanket of white. The pattern of frost on the inside of my window is that of icy white tendrils which look as though they would encircle the whole Manor, if they could. I usually like seeing them, but today I do not see beauty in them, just cold, harsh frost.

The last awakening seemed to really stir a longing in me to remain with Elsie, and the poem she told me, as I left, is still ringing in my ears. I can feel a growing impatience inside of me, and this is not like me at all. During my meeting with Lord Haskell he had told me to expect another awakening soon, but that had taken several weeks to appear. During that awakening Elsie had promised that soon we would no longer have to be apart. But that was now a week ago, how long must I wait before the truth in my heart is unlocked? For now, I am certain that this is what I want, and I know without it, I will never be able to experience any true peace or fulfilment.

Strangely, throughout all this, Miss Florence has continued to be a source of great comfort to me, her friendship is one that I treasure and do not want to lose, no matter what lies ahead for me. I have even begun to think that perhaps she knows more about me, and even the awakenings, than I ever thought she did.

As I dress and ready myself for the day ahead, I cannot help feeling as though perhaps today may bring forth another awakening, although I fear this may not be the one I am waiting for. Certainly, if it is not another awakening, then something is definitely going to happen that will either answer some of my outstanding questions, or else confuse me further, either way I know I have to be ready.

I make my way down to breakfast, and knowing I am up early, expect to be first. However, as I reach as I reach the bottom of the staircase I can already hear voices in the dining room. One is unmistakably Lord Haskell's and another, Lady Haskell's, but the third, although strangely familiar is not one I can place immediately. As I draw nearer to the dining room the unknown voice is making me feel uneasy, even fearful, and I realise now that Lord Haskell's voice is raised and Lady Haskell appears to be distressed. What's wrong? Where is Miss Florence? Who does that voice belong to?

I reach the door of the dining room and am relieved to find it closed; I do not attempt to enter, but remain in the hallway and listen. The raised voices stop and for a few seconds there is silence, but then my fear rapidly increases as steps approach the door. Now the mystery voice is the one that speaks.

'If that is your final word on the matter, then I will take my leave, but this is not yet over. I will return and the girl will see me, and hear all that I have to say to her. Good day Sir, good day Madam, good day Miss.'

Then Miss Florence must also be in there!

The handle of the door begins to turn and I look desperately for somewhere to hide. Seeing nowhere else I move quickly back towards the staircase and slide myself into a narrow alcove in which is a marble pedestal that has a large, ornately decorative vase on top of it. From here I can still see the door; I dare not go in to far for fear of toppling the vase from its resting place, as that would be sure to get the mystery man's attention, for the voice did indeed belong to a man. He's taking forever to open the door, eventually it opens and I see him, the man I had always known as my Uncle, until a few months ago when I discovered the truth, there stood my Father. So it was me he wanted! My legs become weak and my heart pounds, as I watch him searching briefly as he makes his way to the front door; it is almost as though he knows I am here. I hardly dare breathe. At last the huge door opens and an icy blast whips along the hall causing me to shiver. The door closes behind him, but still I am too afraid to move. Several minutes pass, he does not return. Taking great care to not wobble the vase, I leave my hiding place. Instead of going to the dining room for breakfast, I quickly retreat back upstairs to the sanctuary of my room, taking care to lock the door behind me. My breathing is rapid and shallow, I am trembling all over, but at last I am safe. After a few minutes and taking great care not to be seen, I move across the room to the window and try to peer out. The tendrils of frost are still too thick and my view is obscured, at least this means I am not visible to him either. Moving back to the bed, I sit and pull the thick blanket around me. Although there is a roaring fire in the grate, I am still frozen cold. As I try to warm my chilled body, I realise the frost on the window makes no sense, the fire had been lit early when my tea tray was brought up, so the frost should have melted away a long time ago, what is happening here? I wonder, is this an awakening after all? I return to the window a second time, this time my view is clear and in the distance I can just make out a carriage moving slowly and with difficulty away from the Manor. As I sit and watch it make its way with great caution into the distance, the silence is broken by a knock on my door. Although I feel I have been back up here for several minutes, in truth it is more like several seconds and someone must have heard me run back up the stairs. I feel myself tighten all over, as whoever is outside knocks for a second time. Still I dare not answer. A third knock, and this time they speak;

'Ruby, are you alright child? You are quite safe now, he has gone and will not be returning for a long while, that is if he knows what's good for him! Please Ruby, will you not come down with me and have a little breakfast?'

The reassurance in the rich, deep, kindly voice of Lord Haskell seems to calm me almost instantly, so I unlock the door and open it to find him standing, waiting for me. However, he has obviously taken a great dislike to my Father, and I cannot help but wonder whether he is aware of the harshness of Herbert's life.

'Please Sir; do not think too harshly of my Father, his life has been marred with trauma and not at all a happy one. It is true that I am afraid of him, but I would not want any harm to come to him all the same.'

I blurt this out without thinking and only after I have finished do I stop and begin to wonder, how much does Lord Haskell know? Does he even know that he is my Father? I need not have concerned myself as his expression and response assure me that he is indeed fully aware of all the circumstances.

'Your loyalty and understanding do you great credit Ruby, but whatever he has been through does not excuse his bullying, uncaring manner towards you and towards Elsie. If he truly desires to have a relationship with either of you and to get to know you, he has to earn that right by showing an understanding that you both have also suffered trauma and harshness of treatment, and therefore need gentle love and compassion not bullying and dominating! Now, come child and try to eat a little breakfast, it will help you feel better.'

Leaving my room for the second time this morning, it is only as I get halfway down the stairs that a new reality hits me and I stop once more. How much do Lady Haskell and Miss Florence know? They were both present in the dining room this morning while my Father was here; in fact Lady Haskell was also part of the conversation that had taken place. If they know now, how long have they known? Have they always known? If they have, why has Miss Florence never questioned me? Lord Haskell has reached the bottom of the stairs before he realises I am no longer just behind him.

'Ruby, what is it child? Why have you stopped? There is nothing to fear now, and you really do need to eat something child.'

'Please Sir, it is just that I know Lady Haskell and Miss Florence were in the dining room with yourself and my Father earlier, and I am curious. How much do they each know about me and my story? Do they know that Herbert is my Father? Do they know about...?'

'Calm yourself child, lady Haskell knows as much as I do, but Miss Florence only knows as much as she needs too. She is now aware that he is your Father, but does not know about the awakenings, at least, not to my knowledge. When and if you want her to know, is your decision, this is after all your story to tell. Please do try not to worry yourself further, she will not question you or even mention this morning as I have told her that it will only distress you. In truth, I think this whole episode has frightened her, so I don't think she would want to talk about it anyway.'

By the time Lord Haskell has finished speaking I am once more at his side and ready to try to eat some breakfast.

As Lord Haskell has already told me, Miss Florence does indeed appear shaken by this morning's events, and is unusually quiet, even since the change in her attitude. Lady Haskell shows great concern for me, and is more than a little distressed by it all herself too.

With breakfast finally over and the snow falling thick and fast outside, any idea I may have had of a winter morning walk is soon dispelled, and I am soon caught up in the many ideas for indoor activities which are already being suggested. It is Miss Florence who comes up with the idea of designing and making Christmas cards, and this meets with approval all round. In fact, Lady Haskell even says she will join us in this. So the three of us make our way to the front sitting room, and with pencil, charcoal and card begin to sketch, and after only a short while we achieve some very pleasing results. Lord Haskell appears and suggests that perhaps Miss Florence and I might like to write a few lines to go inside. This idea pleases us both, so we begin composing some suitable little verses. We soon get lost in this task and do not even notice that Lady Haskell has left the room with her husband. It is not until she reappears to tell us it is lunchtime that we even begin to realise just how long we have been here.

'Florence, Ruby, are you ready to come through and join us for lunch?'

'Oh Lady Haskell, is it really that time already? It only feels as though a few minutes have passed since we joined you in here after breakfast.'

Lady Haskell smiles and is about to respond, but an impatient Miss Florence quickly jumps in instead.

'Of course it is time for lunch, I'm starving, aren't you hungry Ruby?'

This is the first time in several weeks that Miss Florence has shown this side of her character, and although it has been lovely to be able to get to know the real Miss Florence, something inside me has missed this other Miss Florence and seeing this spark in her again makes me smile. I become aware that all my fear and upset from earlier has left me, at least momentarily. Who would have thought that the craft of card making, and act of writing poetic verses, could be so calming, not to say comforting? Now, I too am feeling hungry, and eagerly make my way to the dining room.

'Yes Miss Florence, I am hungry so what are we waiting for, let's go.'

For the first time since my arrival here, I feel somewhat flighty and frivolous and cannot help giggling to myself at the thought of Matron seeing me like this. For the first time ever my memories of her do not fill me with terror and dread, but with mischievous glee and almost a yearning to do things which I know would cause myself a great deal of punishment, but to her would be a source of great irritation. However, I resist this temptation and content myself with the knowledge that I could do them if I wanted too.

Lunch is soon over and still the snow falling outside, it appears to be in even greater quantities than this morning. I sit staring out at the mesmerising scene, and soon begin to see pictures and other images appear amidst the whiling white crystal flakes. It is this overwhelming silence and beauty which enables me to feel as though I am the only person in the room. Not many minutes pass before I feel as though the window is getting closer and any minute now I will find myself amongst all those tiny dancing figures and part of the picture.

Could this really be an awakening? How can this happen with everyone else watching? Surely this is simply my imagination? I force myself to look away from the window and glance back into the room. Just as I do so Miss Florence's voice breaks through into my dream like state.

'Ruby, are you going to sit here staring out of that window all afternoon, or are we going to do something?'

'Hmm, sorry, what was that? Oh… oh I am sorry Miss Florence I was quite mesmerised by the snow falling outside. What is it that you would like to do?'

As soon as I have finished asking the question I know I am going to regret it.

'Well, I think this is the ideal day to go up and explore the turret room don't you? We can't go outside so we can explore somewhere new in here!'

An icy blast of air rushes past me and I shiver.

'Why Ruby, what on earth is the matter? You look as though you have seen a ghost, don't tell me you are scared of going up there? I have always wanted to see it, and I thought you did too?'

I remain motionless, I know that the icy blast was a reminder of the promise I made to Elsie several months ago. I also dare not stand at the moment, as I fear my legs will not hold me if I tried to leave my seat.

'No, Miss Florence, I am not scared, it is just that it will be much darker and colder up there. As it is locked, perhaps you should consider asking your parent's permission first?'

This attempt to sound confident, brave and in control of the situation is so unconvincing that Miss Florence is bound to find it unacceptable, and pursue her idea with or without me. As for asking her parents, this suggestion is most unlikely to please. Despite my denial, I am in fact terrified and know that to accompany her on her quest will break a solemn promise, and yet to allow her to go alone would be a dereliction of my duty as her companion, I slump forward resting my head on my folded arms on the table in despair. To my astonishment, she simply comes back at me with more questions.

'Is it really locked? How do you know that? Have you already been there without me?'

Relieved a little to still be only talking about the turret room, I respond with a little more confidence than before.

'Only when I first arrived here and was exploring alone one day, I just felt that perhaps it had been locked for a reason, perhaps to contain years of heartache and sadness, or maybe a dark secret that somebody wanted to keep locked away.'

'Oh Ruby, do you really think so? That would be horrible, but why would I not have been told? My parents have always told me I have to be honest, but to keep something like that from me isn't being very honest is it?'

'Miss Florence, please try to understand that it may not be anything like that. Even if it is, perhaps Lord and Lady Haskell have not told you because they are trying to protect you. Sometimes people do not say or do certain things for the best of reasons.'

Miss Florence sits opposite me looking indignant, but also thoughtful. I am still half expecting her to jump up and go to confront her parents immediately, but she doesn't, it is almost as though something is preventing her. It is only now that I realise her parents are no longer with us, and now as I glance once more to the window, the light has all but gone and the dark cloak of night is enveloping the Manor once more. But, I also notice that the snow has stopped falling, the sky has cleared, and the large bright orb of the moon is climbing high into the sky. It is Miss Florence who eventually breaks the silence once more.

'Do you know what the secret is, Ruby? Can you tell me all about it? Then, just maybe I won't want to go up there?'

What can I possibly tell her? I know that room contains something pertaining to my own story, but even I don't know what it is. If I try to explain that I have made a promise to Elsie that I will not go up there, she will insist on being told everything, what am I going to do or even tell her?

It is at this moment Lady Haskell appears and asks to speak with me alone. Miss Florence is not at all happy and cannot understand why she should be excluded from this conversation. I have never seen or heard Lady Haskell raise her voice before, but now this sweet gentle lady leaves her daughter in no doubt that she is not welcome. This dramatic reaction even makes me feel uncomfortable, and I promise Miss Florence that I will rejoin her as soon as I am able too.

Leaving the dining room and a rather frustrated, not to say irate Miss Florence behind, I follow Lady Haskell back across the hall and into the front sitting room we had been in earlier. Still feeling rather anxious and uncomfortable having witnessed Lady Haskell's sharpness towards her daughter, I cautiously take a seat beside the fire when invited to do so.

'Dearest Ruby, I know you met with my husband a few weeks ago and heard a great deal of our story. I also understand that you were able to share with him much of your own. I have asked to meet with you this afternoon because, it is my belief that you may need or want to ask me something, or even just talk to me about anything which may have occurred or has been troubling you since that meeting. So, is there anything you wish to say? Perhaps there is something you wish to ask, maybe beginning with this morning's unfortunate visitor?'

Her voice, once more with its usual gentle, is almost hypnotic, and I begin to relax again. But I am still somewhat taken aback by this sudden meeting with her, and I really cannot think of anything to say. The silence becomes long and awkward, and I begin to feel as though I should say something just to break the silence, but to my relief Lady Haskell is the one to break it and my awkwardness must be more visible that I realise.

'Oh Ruby, I am sorry, I should not have done this without asking you first, I simply wanted to give you the time and space to speak freely without the constant awkward questions, which I know only too well, my daughter is more than capable of asking. Please child, rest assured that whatever we talk about remains between us, and that time is not limited in anyway. Please, take your time, I could see this morning that you had a need to talk, but knew that the time was not available to us then. Now, what is it you wished to say earlier and couldn't?'

'Please Lady Haskell, when I entered the dining room for breakfast this morning I believe that you wished to ask me something, and felt you couldn't because Miss Florence was there, what was it you wished to know?'

Smiling kindly she looks towards me and then towards the door as it opens as a tray of tea is brought in.

'Child, you are much more knowing

and aware than I realised, and for that I apologise. You are quite correct, I did indeed wish to ask you something, or more particularly say something to you, which my daughter would only have questioned. You recognised the voice of your father this morning and were filled with fear, but yet you pleaded with my husband not to judge him too harshly, this indeed does you great credit. However, my husband explained that he should be aware that you and Elsie have also suffered greatly, and as a result should be treated with care and love. Perhaps you wondered why my husband referred to you both in this way and at the same time?'

This thought had not entered my head until now, but now it is whirling around like the snowflakes of earlier.

'Well, I have always known there is a connection between all three of us, at least I have since the awakenings began, and Elsie came back into my life, so I just accepted it and really gave it no more thought. Am I wrong not to question this further Lady Haskell?'

I wait almost awkwardly for a response, and when Lady Haskell turns and looks at me again, I can see in her face a desire to tell me something, but also the knowledge that she cannot.

'Oh Ruby, there is so much more than just a connection between you all, but alas, I am not able to explain further. I know you have made a promise not to enter the turret room, and that you have kept it, despite my daughter's constant pleading and continuous efforts to persuade you to accompany her up there. You are indeed a very loyal and faithful child. It is my belief that your time for keeping that promise is soon to be over, but you must ensure that you are alone when this time comes, or at least not with Miss Florence.

Now, this afternoon when I came back into the dining room, you were still sitting exactly where you had been when we left you. I believe that you may have seen something, and because you were not alone, did not allow it to happen. Am I correct Ruby?'

'Oh Lady Haskell, it is not so much that I saw anything specific, it was really more like a feeling of something being about to happen, like an awakening. However, when I looked away from the window it just stopped and all was as it had been.'

'What made you think or believe something was about to happen Ruby? You must have felt or witnessed something unusual, or was it perhaps a voice you heard?'

It is now that my head begins to whirl and my mind flashes back to something Lady Haskell said a few moments ago about me needing to be away from Miss Florence when the time comes. How can I arrange this, when all the time the weather is preventing me from leaving the house? The only time I am alone is when I am in my room at night. This thought fills me with dread, I have only experienced awakenings at night a few times, and the thought of the Turret Room at night is terrifying. Also, I do not really want to expand or explain the window dream further, as I am not really certain myself of what had occurred if in fact anything had, but Lady Haskell quite obviously knows more than I thought. Did she perhaps also feel or see something earlier? I decide not ask, but to try to explain what I felt had happened.

'Well Lady Haskell, I am so uncertain myself that I do not really want to say, but as you have asked I will try to explain. It was after lunch as we sat at the table that I happened to glance out of the window. I did hope that the snow had stopped and that I would be able to go out for a walk this afternoon, but as I looked it became obvious that it was snowing even faster than this morning. But I soon found that I couldn't look away from it, I became mesmerised, almost enchanted by the dancing figures I was now seeing. It was almost as if I was part of it, then the window appeared to be coming towards me as though I was about to enter a different place, I forced myself to look away and it is then that Miss Florence asked again about the Turret Room, then when I looked again the window was simply showing normal snow falling. Then you entered and you know the rest, but it was only when you re-entered that I even knew you and Lord Haskell had left the room. Please, can you help me to understand what it all means? Do I really have the power to stop an awakening? Is all that I have witnessed and experienced since my arrival here just my imagination? Am I controlling what happens?'

I can say no more as tears are falling and nothing seems to make sense now.

'Hush child, why such great distress? I cannot tell you everything Ruby, but know this;

All that happens is for you,
To help you discover your way through,
All that you see,

The Diary of Miss Ruby March

Is bringing you one step closer to me,
All that you hear,
Need not cause you to fear,
You cannot change what will be,
Only know that you will soon be free.

Please believe me when I say that everything you have experienced and seen here is because of your imagination, it is not in your imagination, it is this gift which enables you to be open to the awakenings. You also need to know that because an awakening did not take place today is not down to you. Sometimes when things try to happen before the time is right it is because we are wanting them so much even if we are not aware of this. So, in this sense you do have some control, however, neither you nor anybody else has any power over whether or not the things we see ever fully make themselves known. This can only happen when everything that needs to be is in the right place. Do you understand this Ruby?'

Still feeling shaky and somewhat overwhelmed by the day's events, I have to admit to Lady Haskell that I don't, but that somehow, now it doesn't seem to matter.

The Diary of Miss Ruby March

7 October 1877

This morning I wake to discover that the snow has started falling again, so any possibility of going outside is a very unlikely one. Usually this would result in me feeling trapped and low, but for some reason this morning it really doesn't matter to me at all. My head is still whirling after meeting with Lady Haskell yesterday afternoon, but even this is no longer a worry to me. In fact, I feel quite at peace with everything. I throw back the bed clothes and then hurriedly pull them back over me again, as the icy air makes my skin tighten all over. I have never felt my room this cold before. Looking across to the fireplace, I can see the fire blazing as usual, so why is the room so cold? The curtains, they are open, of course, that is how I can see the snow has started falling again. But this makes no sense, when I came up to bed last night I know they were closed. I glance at the clock on the mantelpiece. That's strange, the clock says that it is not yet dawn, but the window appears to be showing full daylight.

Gathering a thick woollen blanket around my shoulders I creep out from beneath my covers and across the floor towards the window. Peering out I can see that it is still dark outside, but I can see the falling snow so clearly and room still appears to be flooded with light. Is this an awakening? Is this what I should have seen yesterday? This time it cannot be me just wanting something to happen, as I was fast asleep until just a few moments ago, so what is going on?

I continue to stand and stare out of my window wrapped tightly in the thick blanket, not only for warmth, but also for comfort. I continue to watch, hoping that I will once again see what I did yesterday, but nothing other than the gently falling snow against the inky night sky. After a few minutes my feet are so cold that they have gone numb, and my eyes become heavy and difficult to keep open. So, I turn and begin crossing the floor once more, back towards the bed. It is now that I realise my room has grown dark again and when I get back to my bed, the curtains are again closed and the chill in the air is noticeably less.

Cuddling down once more beneath the layers of covers I shiver, that was so strange, I have not witnessed anything like this before. In spite of my eyes feeling heavy, I begin to doubt very much whether I will sleep properly again tonight. My feeling of peacefulness from earlier is still very much with me, and the next time I open my eyes I glance at the mantel clock, this time I am shocked to find that the clock is indicating that it is already breakfast time and I am now going to be late.

It is only as I try to get out of bed that I realise I am still wrapped in the blanket from earlier. As I fight to free myself and hurriedly wash and dress for breakfast, I hear a gentle, almost timid knock on my door.

'Who is it? Is that you Miss Florence? I am sorry but I overslept, I am coming now, please rest assured that I am quite well and will be with you shortly.'

There is no answer so assume the person has left. However, after a few minutes the knock is repeated. This time I answer the door expecting to find a rather agitated Miss Florence, instead I find Elsie standing there and the rest of the house still in blackness.

'Oh…oh Elsie, you are not who I was expecting. What are you doing here? I thought I was late for breakfast, but it appears I am mistaken. Yet I am certain the clock said…'

'Ssh Ruby, look again.'

I do so without question, I now see that it reads the same time as it did when I first woke up.

'I...I don't understand, what is happening here? Elsie please, what is going on? This feels wrong for an awakening, and yet it must be as nothing else makes any sense.'

'Hush child, this is indeed an awakening but in a slightly different way, our two times are trying to merge, but as yet cannot. This time you decide when it is over, or maybe I should say...'

'Say what Elsie? What did you stop yourself from saying? Also, what do you mean our two times are trying to merge? How could that even happen?'

'None of this matters now, for whatever you decide today will determine the rest of your life and change several others forever. Now, if you are ready, come with me.'

I have never felt less ready than I do right now, nevertheless, I say no more and follow her obediently along the dark corridor towards the back staircase.

'Where are we going? How can we possibly venture outside in weather like this and at night too? This staircase leads to-'

But I can say no more, as I see Elsie has begun climbing upwards, not downwards, and that can only mean one destination. The

Turret Room.
I stop following and remain at the landing.

Elsie has not gone far herself before she realises that I am no longer with her. Retracing her steps to join me once again on the landing, she takes me by the hand.

'Ruby, what is it child?'

She does not pause long for me to respond, but instead smiles knowingly and continues.

'Dearest Ruby, you have been both loyal and trustworthy in keeping your promise to me and have not entered this place, but now the time is right and the last parts of the puzzle can only be unlocked by entering this room, and discovering for yourself the secrets contained within. Are you ready to finally know your whole story so far, discover who you really are, and to determine where it goes from here?'

'Oh Elsie, this is all so sudden, I really don't know if I am ready, in fact, I don't know if I even want to. What if…'

My fear is great and causes my throat to tighten thus preventing me from saying more.

'My sweet child, if you wait until you feel truly ready you will never know the truth, and if you didn't want to know, why have you already come so far along this journey? You are bound to feel anxious, even fearful, but the uncertainty of never knowing is far more destructive and harmful than anything you could discover behind that door. You do still trust me, don't you Ruby?'

'Of course I do Elsie, it is just that-'

'Then you need to come with me and know. Do you understand?'

'Not really, but...but I will go if you come with me?'

'From this point on I can always be with you, but only if this is what you want. Shall we continue?'

No further words are exchanged, but I follow Elsie up the narrow staircase until side by side we are facing the door of The Turret Room. My heart is pounding hard as we approach. I remember suddenly that the door is locked.

'Oh Elsie! This door, the first and last time I came here, it was locked and there is no key. How are we supposed to enter?'

'There was no key because the time was not right, but Ruby, have you looked today?'

I approach the door and see a small silver key hanging on a hook beside the door.

'I...I don't know what to do, and I will always want you with me, you must know that?'

Elsie says nothing but smiles knowingly as she takes the key from its hook and places it in my hand.

'Can't you unlock it for us to enter?'

'No child, this time it must be done by you, only you can unlock the whole story.'

'But…but you will come in with me won't you? You won't leave me to discover this alone will you? Please say you won't?'

Again Elsie smiles and says nothing, only this time it as though she is trying to hide something, is she feeling scared too?

'Open the door Ruby, what happens from now is up to you and you alone.'

With my fingers trembling and my breathing rapid I place the key in the lock and turn it. As I do so, I see a glowing light all around the small dark door, and get the feeling that something is waking from a long, enchanted-like slumber. I place my palm on the handle, and before I even turn it, the door swings open. To begin with the light is so bright I cannot see to enter, by the time I am able to focus on my surroundings, I realise that I am already in the room. I turn to see the door still standing open, and dark corridor beyond, but the room has enveloped me rather than allowing me to enter it. I suddenly panic, where is Elsie? She is no longer with me!

'Elsie, ELSIE WHERE ARE YOU? You promised to stay with me, but you are not here, please come back.'

Frantically I look all around for her, but she is nowhere to be found. I try to make my way back towards the door, to see if she is still in the corridor, but no matter how many steps I take towards it, or how quickly I move, the door never gets any closer. Why can't I see Elsie? Why is she not here with me? Why am I not able to get out of this place?

Feeling isolated and alone, I decide that my only option is to keep going, and as I take a step forward I hear a voice clearly telling me to remember, remember what though?

'Elsie, is that you? Why have you left me here? What is it that you want me to remember?'

The voice does not respond, but as I stand there a memory begins to stir, as though someone has pulled it forward for me to recall. Now I know exactly what it is I have to do. The first piece of advice I was given during only my second awakening, was to keep moving forward and not look back.

Still wishing that I had Elsie at my side, but feeling more certain, I take another step, and another and another. It is not long before the

Turret Room opens out and I find myself surrounded by what, at first glance, appear to be boxes, but on closer inspection I can see that they are tiny models of scenes and…. No, it can't be, each one appears to be depicting an awakening. As I continue to look I realise that they are all here, all locked away in the Turret Room and from the covering of dust, they have been in here a long time. But, the longer I study them the more I realise that something is wrong, something is missing. All the scenes and places are here, but there are no people, none anywhere and a feeling of melancholy hangs above each one. I even find the window from yesterday, but this makes no sense because Lady Haskell had led me to believe that I had only seen what I did because I desperately wanted too. I begin to doubt whether any of them were real, and yet I know deep inside me that they are.

Not daring to even glance behind me, I press on. What's this? A black curtain prevents me from going further, but on it is an envelope. I stop and try to calm myself, but without any success. Trembling all over, I approach the curtain and remove the envelope. I see a table and chair tucked around a corner that I didn't even know were there. The Turret Room is certainly much bigger than I had imagined it to be, but I suppose if time is different during an awakening, size and boundaries don't exist in the same way either.

Taking a seat at the table I stare at the envelope, turning it over and over between my fingers. The only writing on it is my name, and yes, it is in Elsie's own delicate and beautiful handwriting. Why has she left me a letter now? It was only a short while ago, outside this place that she promised we could be together always, but she is not here, and now I find this letter, I don't understand. I know I have to open the letter, but the contents within scare me.

After several more minutes with nothing changing, I slowly begin to lift the flap. As I do so, a growing sense of impending finality grips me, and I know that this envelope contains the greatest secret, and that before I can pass beyond the curtain I must read its content. Do I really want to know? Do I really want to risk changing all this? The truth is I don't know, but I do know that I risk being stuck here, unable to move backwards or forwards if I don't, and this thought scares me even more. So, I lift the flap more quickly now, and begin to read;

The Diary of Miss Ruby March

To my dearest Ruby,

There is a truth so long kept hidden,
But now you need to know,
What was done so long ago,
Was done with a heart so heavy.
Your mother fell in love,
She thought he loved her too,
And though he tried to care and give,
He was not allowed to live that life.
To live a life of his own choosing,
No, he was born to do his duty.
Fearing what may lie ahead,
And desperate to keep you safe,
A life she never wanted,
Was the only way to go.
A life of separation,
But never without love,
Was what tore us apart,
And was the cause of many tears,
Shed over many years,
But when I could,
I kept you close,
When I could not,
I kept you locked,
Forever in my heart of love.
What happens now is up to you,
It is you, who must decide,
But know whichever way you go,
I'll forever be at your side.

'But...but what does all this mean? Oh Elsie, can't you help me? I thought my mother was dead, now reading this I am not so sure, please, help me?'

Hot salty tears blur my sight, but as I sit staring at the lines I have just read, a feeling is stirring within me. I try hard to suppress it, as if it were true, everything I have known for the last year could be lost, but I would gain the one thing I never thought I would have. I feel as though I am at a point where there are now only two clear paths available to me and I have no idea which one I should take.

When I eventually look up from the letter I can see that the black curtain is gone and has been replaced by two doors with a small window between them. I leave my seat at the table and move towards the window. As I look through it all I can see is a signpost with two arrows pointing in opposite directions, apparently one at either door. To begin with I cannot make out what either of them say, but then, a mist starts to clear and the arrows become clearer, I cannot help but let out an audible gasp. The arrow on the right simply reads 'Yesterday' while the one on the left simply reads 'Tomorrow', so which door should I open.

The Diary of Miss Ruby March

I stand looking from one door to the other and back again. If I choose yesterday, does that mean things will stay as they are now, or at least were before I entered here? If so, is this what I truly want? But if I choose tomorrow and everything changes, will I ever be as happy as I have been since my arrival here? Something is telling me that once I have made my choice, the other will simply disappear. I glance fleetingly over my shoulder, but all I see is the black curtain that had been barring my progress is now barring my way back.

'Well, this is it then, I have to choose one of these doors as the only way out of here is to open one, but which one?'

Why I say this out loud I really can't say, there is no-one to hear me, but perhaps I hope it will help me to decide. Once again Elsie's words return to me and I know I must go forward into tomorrow. I look for a handle but find nothing. How am I supposed to open a door without a handle?

I take a step back and immediately doubts and uncertainties flood into my mind. If I take tomorrow's door will I ever return to my life at the Manor? What is to become of Miss Florence and Lord and Lady Haskell? Will the awakenings just stop? But, if I go back to yesterday, maybe the awakenings will stop anyway, and not knowing everything I can about who I really am might be worse? No, I must go forward. Once again I take a step towards the leading to tomorrow, only this time with greater purpose and to my amazement it simply vanishes and I find myself at one end of a long but beautiful path. The sign post, the little window and the other door have all vanished too, so, one step at a time I begin my journey along this pathway. As I do so, something about it becomes more and more familiar, and I am almost certain that I have travelled it before, although at the moment it is as though something or perhaps even someone, is preventing me from knowing exactly when, or more particularly, where it leads.

The path continues, only now I am sure I am going up a hill. Eventually it begins to open out into a rather grand gravel driveway. Now I know I have been here before and it is fear that grips me again as I know, or at least I think I know, what I will find at the end. I stop before I see the scorched, charred shell of the Manor after the fire, as I have no wish to return to a place of such devastation and tormented sorrow. This makes no sense, why would my story be revealed in such a place? I am supposed to be moving towards the future not back into the past, but, when I turn back thinking I must have made a wrong turn, the path is now impassable as it is covered with a tangled mass of ivy tendrils and other overgrowth.

As I continue to stand in this place feeling alone and desperately fearful, I hear something, a voice calling to me, calling my name. It is so faint to begin with that I am certain I must have imagined it, but no, there it is again and again, louder now, it is Elsie. I begin moving forward again, slowly at first, but then faster and with greater confidence, I still feel confused about why I should be coming here. However, I know now that there has to be a reason, and for the first time I begin to feel as though my journey is almost over.

The Manor finally comes into view, but this one is not completely surrounded by thick blankets of crystal-encrusted snow, the scene I find myself in now seems impossible. The almost overpowering fragrance of spring flowers is wonderful, and I begin to feel much less afraid, although I still appear to be alone. Even Elsie's voice has stopped now, so I make my way across the beautifully manicured lawn and position myself on the swing seat. I begin to look all around me, and see in the far corner of the garden a cottage, Elsie's cottage, at last.

I stay seated for a while, just looking and wondering which of these two houses I am expected to enter. When, after several minutes no answer appears to be forthcoming, I get up from the seat and begin making my way towards Elsie's cottage. As I approach the door something about the place feels different, almost expectant yet also a little sad. This atmosphere makes me feel uneasy again, however, I try the door and it opens easily. But this time, unlike my previous visits here; there is no table set for tea, no fire roaring in the hearth; in fact it is as though this darling little cottage has been abandoned. The two arm chairs are where they were on my last visit here, but… I shiver as I realise that nothing here has changed at all, except that the table has been cleared. My mind immediately flashes back to my last visit and the moment I left to return to the Manor. I remember now turning to see Elsie wipe away a single tear from her cheek, what did this mean? What does all that I am seeing now, mean? As I continue to stand here feeling my heart thump and race in my chest, could that really have been the last time I was to see her? No, of course not, I have seen her only this morning, what is going on here? Unable to catch my breath properly and with my head spinning almost as fast as my heart is thumping, I all but collapse into one of the arm chairs and begin to sob.

The feeling I tried so hard to suppress from earlier has returned, and this time will not be pressed down. I am rapidly beginning to understand what the deep truth concealed within my heart is, and it is almost too wonderful to believe, but if Elsie really is my own dear mother, where is she? Why can I not see or hear her now that I know the truth?

With my sobs finally easing I open my eyes and decide that I should return to the Manor, but as I lift my head I realise the chill in the air is fading and a fire is burning once more. I turn to look at the table and see that it too has been set for tea, but still Elsie is not here.

'Elsie, oh Elsie, please come to me now, I know the truth and…'
I stop before finishing the sentence. I know now what I must do, what she is waiting for, yet, do I believe it? I mean really believe it enough to try?

In great fear of being wrong I close my eyes and sit facing the crackling flames in the hearth, taking a deep breath, I speak the words I never thought I would be able to.

'Mother, oh mother, I am your daughter, your own Ruby, please come and find me, I am lost without you.'

I do not have to wait for long, as I feel the fresh spring air flood in, as the door to the cottage opens behind me. Still I dare not open my eyes, but I do not need to as I am soon wrapped in the welcome embrace of the only person I have known all my life, yet never known.

For several minutes no words are spoken, I know that it is not just me who is sobbing now, but my mother, my own mother is also sobbing. After a while the tears begin to dry and the silence is broken by the sweetest voice I have ever heard and known.

'Hush now Ruby, you are safe and we need never be apart from this day on. You have found your way home and we can be truly together. Nothing else matters now.'

I know that what she is saying is true, but I suddenly have more questions than answers in my head, but before I can say anything, Elsie speaks again.

'This morning when I left you at the door to the Turret room, my heart was heavy, I still did not know for certain that you would have the courage to come here alone, I even began to fear we would be parted forever, but something in me allowed you to go, and deep down I believed in you. Ruby, my own dear child, thank you for being brave and trusting in all that you have seen. I knew you could do it, I just hoped that you knew and believed that you could.'

She stops talking and looks at me with such a love that I have only ever dreamed of, that is until now, now, it is no longer a dream.

'What is it Ruby? What is it that you want to ask me?'

With so many questions spinning around in my head, I struggle to know what to ask first. Then I realise that time is no longer an obstacle, so it does not matter where I start as they can, and will all be, answered eventually. So, I decide to ask whatever comes to mind first.

'Oh Els… I mean mother, this is far too wonderful to be true and I still cannot really believe it, but there are some things which I have to know. Please, can you tell me the answers?'

'I will certainly try, but remember you have just unlocked the deepest truth, so search your own heart too and you may find the answers for yourself.'

The Diary of Miss Ruby March

Not really understanding how this could happen, I decide to ask her anyway.

'Please, can you tell me why the weather has changed from winter to spring simply by me coming here? What is to become of my life at the Manor? Are the awakenings going to stop now? Why should this...'

'Hush Ruby, I can only answer one question at a time. Let us begin with your life at the Manor shall we?'

I nod and listen intently to all that she tells me.

'Your life at the Manor will continue, only now we can live it together as mother and daughter, niece and great niece of Lord Haskell. This cottage has only ever been a part of your journey and visible during awakenings. You no longer need it Ruby as you can find all that you need at the Manor. Nowhere is off limits to you now, the Turret room is no longer anymore than an ordinary room and no matter what happens, you are safe.

Like the cottage, the awakenings have served their purpose and are no longer needed, however, never take anything for granted. You may very well still find yourself able to see, hear and experience things that those who are around you cannot. An awakening will only ever be as distant from you as your imagination allows it to be. Never stop believing and living in your imagination Ruby, it is this gift that makes you who you truly are and enabled us to once more be together, it is this which makes you so special. Who knows, one day you too may be called upon to guide someone through their story, as I have guided you, I only pray that it will be for different reasons and without the suffering you have had to endure.

Now, what was your other question?'

I sit motionless and speechless for several minutes before answering, and now I only find myself able to answer with another set of questions.

'Oh mother, please tell me your delightful little cottage will not just disappear, it is a place that I dearly love and want to be able to return forever? What will become of father? Oh yes, my other question, why have we gone from winter to spring, and more importantly how?'

'My dear, sweet Ruby, this cottage will always exist in your heart, and should you ever find the need of such a place again, perhaps when, and if, you should find someone who needs you, then your own place of sanctuary will appear to you, your very own 'cottage'. As for your father, those decisions we will make together, but you have already begun this journey when you pleaded for leniency for him with Lord Haskell, you have already shown more love for him than you could know.

Now, about the weather, what makes you think the seasons have changed, you forget that you haven't been outside today, you only entered a room inside the Manor. Why don't you open the door?'

'What are you telling me mother? Are you saying that we are still in the Turret room that simply isn't possible, is it?

'Why don't you just open it and see for yourself, remember this is still an awakening?'

A cold shiver races through me as I hear those words. If this is only an awakening then is any of this true or real? I approach the door of the cottage, but dare not turn the handle.

'What is it child? Trust your heart and it will never fail you or let you down.'

With my heart once more throbbing, partly still with fear but mostly with a real sense of hope for a future I never thought I would have, my hand trembling, I turn the handle and open the door.

To begin with it as though my eyes are closed, but gradually they adjust and I realise that I am once more gazing into the dark corridor outside the Turret room, only this time as I stand there I feel my mother's hands take hold of my own and I know she is coming too.

'Are you ready Ruby, this morning we will all have breakfast together?'

This morning a life I never believed I would know can really start, and I know for the first time why I had to promise not to enter the Turret room. This was Elsie's place.

Dear Reader
If you have enjoyed reading this book, then
please leave a review on Amazon.
Thank you.

About the Author

Elizabeth Manning-Ives is the pen name of published poet Helen Thwaites and `The Diary of Miss Ruby March' is her fourth novel. Her first three `Living Under the Shadow', 'A Journey of Significance' and 'When Tomorrow Comes' have all received 4 and 5 star reviews on Amazon.

As well as writing, Helen also enjoys a variety of handicrafts, nature and playing the flute. In the past she has also been involved with many amateur dramatics productions locally. She is heavily involved with her church and a local choir. She loves chocolate and insists that it stimulates and enhances her writing.

Printed in Great Britain
by Amazon